Gore Orphanage

A novel based on the feature film

Emily Lapisardi

Gore Orphanage

First Edition

Gore Orphanage is a work of fiction. Names, characters, places, and incidents are the products of the author's imagination or are used fictitiously.

Photographic illustrations courtesy of Principalities of Darkness, LLC (photographers Sabrina Mangin, Ray Wade, and Nicholas Carrington)

Brandon Mangin, Jr. as Buddy, Nora Hoyle as Esther,
and Emma Smith as Nellie

I.

Ted took his daughter Amber's hand as they walked down the hallway of the nursing home. They had told him that his grandmother was being moved to a rehabilitation facility, but the residents in this place seemed to be waiting to die, not to return to their previous lives. In room after room, they passed fragile, wizened figures covered in cold white sheets. Most seemed asleep or unconscious. An odor of decay mingled with the scent of disinfectant.

Amber clutched her teddy bear more tightly as she tried to peer into each room. Grandma Nellie had given her the bear shortly before the fall that had brought her to this facility, and it had quickly become Amber's constant companion, as it had once been her great-grandmother's during her own childhood. Bright eyes still peered out from beneath the matted, faded fur.

"I want to throw that thing away sometime when she's at school," Ted's wife, Sarah, had complained, not long after Amber had received the dubious gift. "It's disgusting. Who knows where it's been. It is probably infested with dust mites, if not fleas." Sarah's relationship with Ted's family had been strained even before their marriage and Grandma Nellie's gift, like Grandma Nellie herself, was something of an embarrassment. The traumas of their long lives were too visible, too scarring.

"Are we almost there, Daddy?" Amber asked, squeezing his hand.

"Just at the end of this hallway, sweetie. She will be so happy to see you."

"And Bear!" Amber added. She was a beautiful girl, with long blonde hair which Sarah made certain was always immaculately styled. As usual, Amber's barrettes coordinated perfectly with her outfit. Ted had been in his forties when he finally married, and Sarah was nearly twenty years his junior. Their only child was the center of his world now. Their home was filled with photos of Amber and of the family together—picture-perfect, beautiful, immaculate. Grandma Nellie was not in those photos.

Amber ran ahead into Grandma Nellie's room, throwing her arms around the old woman in the bed.

"Amber, dearie!"

Grandma Nellie kissed the smooth, pale forehead of the little girl, and then the nose of the proffered bear.

"Find me the zapper, honey, and I'll shut this off." The TV, mounted high on the wall opposite the bed, was blaring a game show.

Amber looked on the nightstand and then, crawling on her knees, under the hospital bed. She emerged with the remote control and smudges of dust on her leggings.

"Dust your pants off," Ted chided, "We don't want Mommy to wonder what you've been up to."

"She's a child, Theodore," Grandma Nellie replied, curtly. "Will anyone let her act like one before she grows up?"

Amber half-heartedly attempted to wipe off her knees, then clambered onto the bed. "How are you, Grandma Nellie? Are you feeling better? Will you be coming home soon?"

"Getting there," the old woman responded, stroking the child's head. "No thanks to this place. I could hardly sleep at night from all the noise while that other bed was occupied. They'd better not fill it right away or I'll never have a chance to get well."

"Did Stella go home?" Ted asked. The last time he'd visited, Grandma Nellie had had a roommate, a silent, mummified-looking woman whose bedside table had been filled with cards, flowers, and balloons. Now, that side of the room was sterile and empty.

5

"No. She died."

Amber looked at the empty bed now, a slight frown creasing her brow. She had never really known death, unlike Grandma Nellie, who had been an orphan by the time she was Amber's age. For Grandma Nellie, death had been a constant companion.

"The food is trash, too," Grandma Nellie continued, matter-of-factly, "It's all mush. I'm the only one with choppers here." She gnashed her teeth at Amber, who giggled, then leaned in and whispered "We'll bring you a chocolate bar next time." Despite her doctor's warnings to limit her sugar consumption, Grandma Nellie was a chocoholic. Since she had moved in with them, Sarah had discovered hoarded candy bars in her room more than once.

"With nuts?"

"Any kind you want, Granny."

"I called Mom." Ted said. "She was worried about you."

"Not worried enough to call me," Grandma Nellie responded.

Ted's mother had been born when Grandma Nellie was still in her late teens, still trying to sort herself out after years of shuffling from one home to another. Their relationship had been strained as long as Ted could remember.

"When you're home, she wants us all to get together," Ted countered. "It's been too long."

"We'll see," Grandma Nellie replied, a strange twinkle in her pale blue eyes, "We'll see if it suits her then."

"Want me to brush your hair, Granny?" Amber asked, pulling a plastic hairbrush from the drawer of the nightstand. It had become their ritual in these last few weeks since Grandma Nellie had broken her hip.

"Of course, dearie. I want to look my best for all of my gentleman callers." She gave Ted an ornery wink.

Amber began to comb through the matted portions of Grandma Nellie's short silvery hair gently and lovingly, stroking the locks with her small, tapered fingers. "I'll bring you hairbows next time, too. What color do you want, Granny?"

"Blue," said Grandma Nellie, "My ribbons were always blue, to go with my eyes. Ask Teddy, he remembers."

She wasn't talking about her grandson.

II.

Mrs. Baker

Those people next door had always been a little strange, and we'd never had much dealings with them since they moved in. You could hear the man practicing his music at all odd hours, and the children were so much younger than Margaret and Kenneth that they hardly ever played together. At first, it was just the father, the boy, and the girl. His wife had died long before, he said, in one of the few real conversations we'd ever had, but he thought the children needed a woman in their lives, the daughter especially. She was a striking-looking little girl, with those dark curls and her big blue eyes, and always clutching the teddy bear. The boy's great joy in life was waiting for the mailman, who often seemed to have a picture postcard for him from some far-away uncle.

About a year after they moved in, we began to see the young woman visiting, and then he married her. She was always well-dressed, with quite a wardrobe of hats and gloves. I never even learned her name. We weren't particularly neighborly by then, and they always kept to themselves.

My son Kenneth was the first to notice something was wrong. "He hasn't been playing the trombone, Mother." Margaret added that she hadn't seen any of them in days. We were at church when they brought it up, so I asked Mr. and Mrs. Dudley, who lived on the other side of them, if they'd noticed anything odd.

"Come to think of it, I haven't seen hair nor hide of them," Mr. Dudley said.

"O dear," Mrs. Dudley added, raising her gloved hand to her lips, "We ought to drop in later." I felt my stomach drop just looking at her. Something was most definitely wrong, but nothing could have prepared us for what we found.

We all went together, the Dudleys, my children, and I. Kenneth rang the doorbell, knocked, and shouted. There was no response, so he and Mr. Dudley pushed the door in.

We had hardly taken more than a few steps into the entry hall when we saw the wife, sprawled on that staircase I had always so envied. There was no question she was dead. There was no blood, no sign of violence, but there she lay, her face on the first landing, dressed in blue velvet as if ready to go out visiting.

The Dudleys pushed forward into the library, but Kenneth raced up the stairs. Margaret and I stood rooted there, staring at the woman. The seams in her stockings were perfectly straight, her nails were manicured, her hair coiffed.

"Up here!" I heard Kenneth cry, and we all followed him upstairs.

I never saw the father or the boy. The father they found in the bathroom, lying in his own vomit. The boy was in his bed, surrounded by his postcard collection. The remains of the dinner that had killed them all was still on the table.

It had become a house of the dead. Try as I might, I have never been able to erase what we saw there from my mind. Margaret was sick that day, and for many afterwards, from the horror of it all.

On the third floor, under the eaves, in a bare little room with flowered sheets, we finally found the girl. She was sitting on the edge of her bed, silent and still. Heaven knows how long she had been there.

"Nellie, are you all right?" I asked. She didn't respond. We had to get her out of there, away from that terrible place. Margaret and I tried to hurry her from the room, but she began to struggle and cry.

"My bear, my bear!"

Margaret found the scruffy teddy on a high shelf. It was the only toy in her room.

There was no other way out of the house except past the body of her stepmother on the stairs. We should never have let the poor child see it. If any of us had been thinking clearly, perhaps we would have thought to ask Mr. Dudley to move the corpse away, but we were all so shocked, so filled with revulsion and a desire to take little Nellie away from those scenes of horror.

I hurried her down as quickly as I could, but she stared at the body and glanced back as the door closed on her old life. Thank God she never saw the others.

Nellie told me later that her stepmother had sent her to bed without supper that day because she had misbehaved. That punishment saved her life. As far as anyone could determine, the tinned beef the rest of the family had eaten was bad and they all died of it, probably very quickly.

I brought Nellie home with us at first. The poor girl had nowhere to go, nothing to her name except her teddy bear and the clothes on her back. She was starving, and ate as much as Kenneth, if not more, at that first dinner. She was never able to tell us how long she had been locked in her bedroom, but it must have been at least a day or two.

Margaret tried to take charge of little Nellie, but the day had been tremendously difficult on my daughter. She had always been a fragile and sensitive girl, and she couldn't swallow a bite of her meal out of fear that she would end up like the neighbors. The ordinary, the innocent, had suddenly acquired the potential to be deadly.

Kenneth, on the other hand, was angry, believing somehow that he might have saved the family if he'd told me sooner that something seemed out of the ordinary. He left on his bicycle after supper, brooding and tense.

Did it ever cross my mind that I ought to raise the child? In hindsight, perhaps, but not then. We hardly knew any of them, and they had always been a bit odd. Her grief frightened me. My husband had been gone just under three years, and my own children were finally beginning to reach a point of normalcy again. Times were hard, too, in our home, and we were barely making do with just the three of us.

Mr. Dudley asked around, but they seemed to have had no family except that uncle who had sent the boy all the postcards, and he was in Austria. There was only one place for the girl to go—the orphanage.

We bought Nellie a few changes of socks and underwear, and Margaret packed them in her own little red suitcase with the elephant on it. She had always loved that suitcase. I was very proud of her charity towards the little orphan girl. Margaret gave her one of her outgrown hats, as well, and I drove Nellie down the long and winding road, over the bridge, to the Francis Gore Memorial Orphanage.

We had all known Mr. Gore, a truly model citizen who, having been orphaned himself as a boy, resolved to aid the destitute children of his adopted land once he had made his fortune. I still remember him, with his waxed moustache and shiny shoes, playing with us at the Fourth of July picnic as if he were one of the children, too. I must have been about ten or eleven then. His own son and daughter had always been a bit aloof, but he was such a kind man, and so interested in all the little details of our childish lives. He brought the orphans to the picnic, and we all ran and rolled down the hill together.

Mr. Gore had been dead a good ten years or more when I took Nellie to the orphanage. I had phoned to tell them we were coming. Mr. Gore's daughter, Victoria, explained everything to me and assured me that taking Nellie there was the best, and only, option for the poor girl.

I took Nellie's hand as we walked towards the house. Mr. Gore had built a true mansion for the orphan children out of great blocks of stone and with a splendid portico. Two girls, twins from the look of them, with neatly braided hair, and matching dresses, watched us approach, then ran off. They seemed like happy, well-kept children, but I saw Nellie clutch her bear a little closer. We climbed the steps to the front porch and I had hardly rung the doorbell when the door opened.

I hadn't seen Victoria Gore in years, but I would have recognized her anywhere. Her wedding picture in the newspaper when she married Captain Pryor had been the envy of many for the opulence of her splendid gown, which the accompanying notice proudly announced had been made in Paris. Captain Pryor had died in the war, though, not long afterwards and Victoria, left childless, had joined her father in caring for the orphans.

She took us into her office, which was tastefully decorated, with very fine orange chairs and a large gilded mirror. Nellie, who had been rather withdrawn at our home, suddenly became very inquisitive, speaking out of turn to ask Mrs. Pryor about the other children. My own children had been taught manners from an early age and would never have been so forward, but perhaps Nellie had not been raised to be polite. I made apologies for her, but Mrs. Pryor was wonderfully understanding. She bent towards Nellie, smiling.

"There are seventeen boys and girls here," she responded, "A few are true orphans like yourself, but many came to us because their parents can no longer care for them since the great crash." I hadn't realized that—there must be more need now than ever for Mr. Gore's charity to extend to destitute children who, though not orphaned, had no other means of food and shelter.

She invited Nellie to stand near the wall, then took her photograph.

"Smile, sweetie, you're about to start a wonderful adventure," she said, and Nellie, still clutching her bear, did manage a slight smile. I hoped that Nellie's new life would be all that Mrs. Pryor claimed, that the child might be able to put tragedy behind her and blossom in this new home.

Nellie had inherited very little after the family's remaining debts and burial costs were paid, but the remainder, paltry as it was, had been forwarded to the orphanage for Nellie's care. Mrs. Pryor sent the child out into the hallway while we discussed the financial details, then assured me that all of Nellie's needs would be met. She would learn a trade so that, when she was too old to remain there, she would be able to support her own needs. I left a few dollars for Nellie personally—I could do no more for the child, and even this was a sacrifice for us. Mrs. Pryor assured me that Nellie would have her own separate account. I do hope they bought her a few more dresses. We could never bear to go back to her house to gather up anything more.

We went out into the hall, where a janitor was working to keep the floor scrupulously clean, and I said goodbye to Nellie. Her eyes were sad, and a little frightened, but I had done all I could for the child. I could not keep her, she had no family, and I believed that the orphanage would be her best chance.

Had I ever guessed what would befall those children, I would have taken her to the ends of the earth to find any other home for her. But how could any of us have ever anticipated that no bright future awaited those poor children, whose lives had already been touched by tragedy? I am haunted by them, too, as well as our neighbors, Nellie's family. I cannot forget; I cannot forgive myself.

Esther

The bed next to mine had been empty for a long time, since Gracie left, and I never slept very well without her there. Gracie had been like an older sister to me since I came to the orphanage when I was a very little girl, four years ago. She taught me how to get to use the bathroom, even in the morning when everyone else wants to, how to pass bed inspection, and what to do when the food is really icky. I cried a lot when I first came, and Gracie wiped my face and hugged me whenever I needed it—which was all the time. My mommy and daddy couldn't take care of me anymore. There wasn't any food to eat, and we lost our house. Mommy said she would come back for me, but she hasn't. I never really thought she would.

I was already half asleep when the door creaked open and I heard Mrs. Pryor's voice. There was somebody new, and it sounded like she was talking to a girl because she called her "Nellie." I tried to pretend I was still asleep, lying in bed on my back with my hands on top of the sheets, just as Mrs. Pryor requires, but I was so excited. There was only one open bed for a girl, the one next to mine.

Mrs. Pryor told her all about bed inspection and the sleeping rules. I listened to every word, though I had heard it all many times before since I came to the orphanage.

"Lights out is promptly at 8 p.m. Children must sleep on their backs with their hands above the covers. They cannot leave their beds until morning and then they must rise at once for bed inspection. There is your bed."

I heard footsteps approaching, nearer and nearer, then the sound of the sheets rustling as she climbed into bed.

As soon as Mrs. Pryor left, I just had to sit up and wave to Nellie. We couldn't talk. It's against the rules to talk after lights out, but I waved to her to let her know how happy I was that she was there. She looked a little older than me, with such pretty dark hair tied back in blue ribbons and a clean white dress. She even had a teddy bear, which she held close. It was hard to go to sleep at first because I was so excited about Nellie, but when I did finally drift off, I slept sounder than I had since Gracie left. I dreamt of soft music, and of happiness.

When Mrs. Pryor woke us for bed inspection, I could only whisper "good morning" to Nellie and show her how to stand next to her bed with the sheet drawn back as Mrs. Pryor made her rounds. She passed through the girls' side of the room quickly, but I could hear that there was a problem beyond the partition, on the boys' side, even though I couldn't see what was happening. It was Ralph again.

William Sutherland IV as Ralph and Wyatt Sutherland as an orphan

"Ralph is a bedwetter," I heard Mrs. Pryor say, and the boys all shuffled into place. Ralph had only been with us a little while, since his grandfather, who was raising him, had died. You could tell from his clothes that Ralph used to have a good life. His hair had grown

15

longer since he had been at Gore Orphanage, but he still tried to dress well, even wearing his striped silk necktie. He was a nice boy, but the older ones—Harmon especially—just couldn't leave him alone about wetting the bed, which only made it happen more. We had to go punish Ralph, too, so I showed Nellie how to roll up her towel and we fell in at the end of the long line. Her face was empty, expressionless. She probably didn't understand what was happening, or what we had to do.

"Don't hit him hard," I whispered, "but make it look like you do."

"Bedwetter, bedwetter!"

Mrs. Pryor began the chanting and everyone joined in, some of the older boys practically screaming as Ralph was made to walk down the row while we smacked him with the towels.

"Bedwetter, bedwetter!"

I could see that Ralph was trying not to cry. Harmon smacked him hard with the towel and Ralph's face crumpled. Harmon's best friends, standing beside him, pummeled Ralph just as hard. Even Buddy, his face set like a mask, swung his towel with a snap. Buddy is my best friend. His name is really Salvatore, but nobody calls him that. All his family in America died and his grandma in Italy couldn't pay for him to go on the boat, so he got stuck in the orphanage.

"Harder, harder!" Mrs. Pryor called out, "Ralph is a bedwetter, children!"

He was coming to the girls now, but Anna hit him just as hard as the boys. Ralph's face had gotten redder and redder, and when Anna's towel flew across his face, the tears finally came.

"Bedwetter, bedwetter," we all chanted, except Nellie. Mrs. Pryor was walking along, making sure that we were punishing him properly, so I glanced at Nellie, who still seemed dazed. She swung

16

her towel softly, barely tapping Ralph, but I gave her a look and she hit him harder the second time.

Nobody likes to punish bedwetters, especially when they're nice, like Ralph. Actually, most of them are. We all know that we have to do it, though, or Mrs. Pryor will punish us too. She made Tommy stand on top of a stool for hours once because he didn't hit Ralph hard enough. I had to make sure Nellie hit him. It doesn't matter if it is your first day or not. You have to learn to behave at Gore Orphanage.

After Mrs. Pryor was gone, we all hurried to get ready before breakfast. I finally could talk to Nellie a little.

"I'm Esther. Is your name Nellie?"

She nodded, hugging her bear.

"Do you need to go to the bathroom?" She shook her head no, but I knew better. "You have to go now, even if you don't feel like it. You won't get another chance until after work."

She didn't answer.

"Bring your towel and come with me. There's only one bathroom for all of us, but I will make sure you get a turn." Slowly, cautiously, she followed. She'll learn.

Harmon sat on the edge of his bed, tying his shoes, as we walked by. His eyes narrowed as he saw Nellie and I tried to hurry her past. Harmon's trouble if you're not a big boy.

Nellie sat beside me at first shift breakfast, too. It was a sunny morning, and the light came streaming through the bay window in the dining room. I saw Nellie look at the artwork on the walls—the words "light" and "hope" with doves and sunbeams—but she still didn't say anything.

Mrs. Pryor read the Bible to us before we ate, like she always does, and I showed Nellie how to fold her hands and bow her head. Maybe she picked the story for Nellie, because it was about bears, but it was a sad story. Mrs. Pryor likes to read all the sad stories in the Bible. My mommy used to read other stories to me, but maybe her Bible was different.

"And he went up from thence unto Bethel: and as he was going up by the way, there came forth little children and mocked him, and said unto him, 'go up thou bald head;' and he turned back, and looked on them, and cursed them in the name of the Lord and there came forth two she bears out of the wood, and tare forty and two children of them." Mrs. Pryor paused. We're supposed to reflect on the verse when she pauses. "The Word of the Lord," she concluded, and we all said "Amen."

Maria Olsen as Mrs. Pryor

It was mush again this morning, and Nellie didn't quite seem to know what to think about it. You get used to eating it after a few days because there isn't much choice, but Nellie wasn't that hungry yet, I guess. She just pushed it around on the plate with her fork.

"I really like your bear," I told her, and she looked at me as if I might take it from her. I can't really blame her. Some of the others might try, especially Harmon, especially if he thought it would make her cry.

"I've never had any toys of my own," I told her, "Did your parents give you that bear?" Nellie nodded sadly. I wonder what happened to her parents. Did they drop her off, like mine did, or were they dead? I could see it meant a lot to her, so I had to warn her.

"Just be careful."

"Why?" she asked. I was glad to hear that she could actually talk, but before I could answer, Mrs. Pryor came up behind us and told us to go to work. None of us girls mind going to work because it means we get to spend the morning with Miss Lillian. Since Nellie and I had first shift breakfast, we would have a longer work day today, but that was just fine by me.

Miss Lillian was waiting for us in the workroom, with the tools already on the table and hot coals glowing in the brazier. Some of the older girls were finishing a couple of quilt tops at the high desk, but the smaller ones, like Nellie and me, were all at the flower table.

Miss Lillian was wearing her pretty blouse with the embroidered roses. It is one of my favorites, but I just love all of her clothes. When I grow up, I want to dress like her. Maybe she will give me some of her old clothes when I am bigger.

Nellie sat her bear down on the window seat beside her as Miss Lillian told us that a new flower order had come in. The girls all know how to make silk flowers, and some of them look just like real flowers. The roses and daisies are my favorites. I'm best at cutting because I am careful and follow the lines.

Every morning, one of us gets Miss Lillian her coffee. Before she could even ask for a volunteer, Anna had her hand up, but Miss Lillian asked Nellie to do it because she is new, and me to help her. I hadn't gotten Miss Lillian's coffee in over a week, and this day was especially important because I got to teach Nellie how.

The coffee pot is always on the table by the lamp with the chubby angels around its base. We got one of the white cups out of the big cabinet and I showed Nellie how to carefully pour it.

"She seems nice, but sad," Nellie said, looking at Miss Lillian.

"She was supposed to get married, but he abandoned her," I said very softly. It's not polite to gossip.

"Why?"

"Spanish flu. It made her barren."

Nellie carried the coffee over slowly and carefully to Miss Lillian, then we sat down at the table again. Nobody had taken the goffering seat, so Nellie was going to have to learn that.

Making silk flowers isn't hard, if you're careful, and there are lots of good jobs for girls. First, you trace the patterns on the right color silk. Always make the leaves green, unless you are making mourning flowers. Then, cut out the pieces along the lines very carefully. Then, depending on what kind of flower you are making, you can paint the edges of the petals. Roses look really pretty, and just like they came from a garden, when you paint them. Then, you use the goffering irons to shape the petals. There are lots of irons, and they all have to be kept hot in the coals until you need them. The ones with the balls are for rounding petals, like roses, and the pointy ones are for creasing petals, like daisies, and making veins in leaves. There are different sizes and shapes for each kind of flower. Somebody has to make the stems, too, wrapping the wire with green ribbon, unless you are making mourning flowers. Then, you glue the petals around the stamen, if your flower has this, and onto the stem.

If you're making daisies or black-eyed susans, somebody has to make the puffy middle part out of thread. Once everything is put together, including the leaves, you hang them up until all the glue dries.

Miss Lillian showed Nellie how to hold the iron to crease the petals of a daisy. At first, she wasn't doing too well. A couple of the daisies will probably look like they are wilting, but if you put them with some really good ones, it will be hard to notice. Nellie started to get it, but was going too fast. You can't rush on flowers, especially goffering. Her hand slipped, and she burned her finger. I tried not to peek, but it looked bad. Anna was sitting beside me and started laughing. She likes it when people mess up, especially new girls. I guess she forgot that she was bad at making flowers when she came.

Nellie was crying and clutching her hand as Miss Lillian rushed over. She put her arm around Nellie.

"Let's get you fixed up," she said, and Nellie took her bear as they left the workroom.

We all tried to go back to work, but I could hear Nellie and Miss Lillian walking down the hallway to Mrs. Pryor's office. The sound of the typewriter stopped, then I heard Miss Lillian talking to Mrs. Pryor and Mrs. Pryor responding. The words weren't exactly clear, but I could tell Mrs. Pryor was angry. Nellie started crying louder.

When she came back, Nellie didn't have her bear.

"What happened?" I asked.

"She took my bear," said Nellie, between sobs, "And she blew cigarette smoke in my face." She coughed softly.

Mrs. Pryor smokes a lot. I could smell the cigarettes on Nellie.

"How is your hand?"

Nellie shrugged, but bit her lip.

"She didn't even look at it. Told me to run cold water on it."

"Why did she take your bear?"

"She said I had to be punished."

"Because you had an accident?"

"Because I didn't work fast enough."

"We'll get it all done, Nellie. I'll help you."

Anna was watching us. She was still smiling, and it wasn't a friendly smile. I gave her a mean look so that she would leave Nellie alone, then started helping with the goffering. I had already cut out fields of daisies.

Mrs. Pryor left in her car before dinner, so Miss Lillian gave us each a roll and let us eat wherever we wanted. I found Buddy and Nellie and I sat with him on the window seat on the main staircase, below the stained glass window. I think the lady in the window was supposed to be Mrs. Pryor, but it sure doesn't look like her. I told Buddy what had happened to Nellie's bear. She should have been more careful. Nobody ever has toys for long.

"My stuff doesn't get taken," he told her, then showed her his secret hiding place. Buddy must really like Nellie. Only his very best friends, like me, know that he keeps his baseball cards wrapped up in his handkerchief under the pipe in the window seat. Buddy's daddy gave him those cards and he loves them more than anything. We sat together as he showed each one of them to Nellie.

"This is my favorite," he said, and showed us a chubby man squatting down.

"He's a fatty!" I said.

22

"A fatty named Gabby," Nellie added, reading the player's name, Gabby Hartnett. We were looking at the cards and didn't notice Harmon coming up the stairs until it was too late.

"What you got there, Buddy?"

"Nothing," Buddy said, trying to hide his cards behind his back. Harmon reached for them, but just then, Miss Lillian appeared.

"Is there a problem here?" she asked, looking right at Harmon. Everybody knows that, if there is a problem, it is usually Harmon.

"No, ma'am," we all said.

"Good, then off to bed," Miss Lillian told us. Buddy slipped his cards back under the pipe as Harmon turned to go up the stairs.

Nellie couldn't go to sleep that night because she didn't have her bear. I tried to sing her a lullaby, but it only made her cry more. I had seen her bear sitting on Mrs. Pryor's office mantle when we went past earlier. The bear looked really sad, like it missed Nellie a lot. It probably couldn't sleep without her, either.

The next day, Miss Lillian let us go out to play when our shift was over. We could hear the voices of the boys out in the woods, setting traps with Ernie. He teaches them how to catch animals for fur and food. Sometimes they go fishing, too, but the girls aren't allowed to go down by the water very often anymore, not since Mary Ellen fell in. The older girls go there to do the wash sometimes, but mostly they just throw our socks and skivvies in when they're boiling corn or potatoes.

Nellie and I were sitting on the steps when Miss Lillian came out of the house with Nellie's bear and gave it back to her. Nellie hugged it tight and I think she and the bear were both smiling.

Anna was jumping rope nearby, her blonde braid and the little cross she always wears bouncing in rhythm. When she saw Nellie had the bear, she came over toward us.

"Esther, Esther, Esther is a pester."

I don't know why she always has to make fun of my name like that. I'm not a pester. Anna is, and sometimes I really hate her.

"Stop that!" I told her, but it only made her smile.

Ryan Nogy as Anna

"Esther is a pester!"

Nellie put her arm around me and held me close. Miss Lillian noticed I was crying and came over. Anna acted as if she was going to leave us alone, but then picked up her jump rope and started skipping again with a big sunny smile. Then, she started to sing.

"I had a little bird. Its name was Enza. I opened the window, and in-flu-enza!"

Miss Lillian stared at Anna, then turned and ran into the house, but I could see that she was crying. I really hate Anna. I hope she gets the influenza and dies, the sooner the better.

III.

Sarah

Sometimes I wonder if Ted was switched at birth. I love my husband, but I don't understand how such a wonderful man could come from such a dysfunctional family and why he feels such loyalty to them. Grandma Nellie should be living in a facility, not with us. We don't have the time or resources to give her the care she needs, and she doesn't make it easy. Not only is she demanding, but she lies and steals.

Ted makes excuses for her. "She was an orphan, Sarah. Her life has never been anything but hard, and she had to be a fighter to survive. You do remember that she was the only survivor of Gore Orphanage, don't you?"

That one always gets me. I don't know how she's managed to convince them all of that wild tale. Gore Orphanage never existed. It's just a story that teenagers tell to scare each other. There were never any children who died in a fire there, and they certainly don't haunt the woods.

When I was younger, I believed the stories, too, or at least wanted to. When you're sixteen, you want to be scared. You seek the unknown, even the dangerous, to prove that you are tough enough to handle it. It's half-fun, half a rite of passage.

We used to go down there, over the bridge, down the winding road, as the sun was setting. We'd tramp through the woods, carrying a cooler of something we were too young to drink, pointing our flashlights left and right at every creaking branch or flying night bird. We knew we would be in deep trouble if our parents found out—drinking, trespassing, making out. You'd hold your boyfriend even tighter as the fear and alcohol made your heart pump harder and your palms sweat. Somebody would swear they'd seen a little ghost boy running through the trees just ahead, but I never saw it.

26

Somebody would feel a little hand pulling at their clothes, but all I ever felt were the mosquitos eating me half to death.

The ruins of the old house smelled like charred wood. The outline of the foundation was still visible, and one of the pillars of the old front gate. There had most definitely been a fire, but anybody who'd ever bothered to check into the story knew that no orphans had died there. Maybe there was an orphanage once, and maybe there'd been a fire, but not when the house was occupied.

The real story was sad—a family struck by illness, losing several children in quick succession, but those things happened frequently back then. It was nothing special, nothing to merit the reputation the spot had gotten over the years.

Once, one of my friends found a little cross pendant half-buried amidst the moss and rubble within the walls of the old foundation. Just outside, they discovered a couple of old bones, too—maybe a deer or a raccoon, who knows—but she was sure she'd found the remains of one of the kids. She was definitely drunk, and probably high.

I never went back after Heather died. It was probably the third or fourth time we'd gone out there: Heather, her boyfriend Dan, Kevin, and me. Heather was obsessed with that place, with the ghosts, and the legend, and especially the story that the children's handprints would show up on your car. Heather had just gotten a car and she and Dan had driven out there together instead of coming with Kevin and me.

"I'm never gonna wipe off the handprints, Sarah," she said, "I'll show them to everyone and then they'll believe me." She was already slurring her speech. I drank a little when we went out there, but never as much as Heather. "You'll believe me. I know you don't, but they're real. I've seen them. I feel them."

She crashed the car on the way home. Dan broke his leg and a couple of ribs, but Heather's neck snapped on impact. They said it happened so fast that she wouldn't have suffered. The whole school was broken up about it. People who barely knew her were crying and carrying on as if they were her closest friends. They brought in special grief counselors, and we were allowed to leave class and go talk to them, but I never did. She was my best friend, and she was dead because of that place, because of our stupidity.

That's why I can't stand it when Ted talks about Grandma Nellie surviving Gore Orphanage. I have even printed out the real story, which thoroughly debunks everything, and given it to Ted, but he doesn't listen to me because his mother, who won't even speak to her own mother, told him. It's their family story, and he wants to believe.

"People want to forget," he says. "It's easier for the community to deny that any of it ever happened rather than remembering that all those unwanted children died a horrible death out there in the woods. But she was there. She hardly ever talks about it, but she remembers. You can't even imagine what a trauma like that does to somebody, especially a little girl who had already lost all of her family. How do you think all the stories developed? Some people do remember, and they talk, even when they are supposed to stay silent."

Supposedly, that disgusting bear of hers survived the fire, too. I don't believe it's really that old. She probably picked it up at some flea market or thrift store and started spinning her stories about it so that she would have something special to give Amber. I have washed it over and over, but nothing will clean it up.

I hate the sway she has over my daughter. Amber is too trusting, and soaks in everything she tells her, her eyes wide. When I try to confront her with the facts, she refuses to admit that she's lied.

"The truth is what we remember," she says, and no matter how much I remind Amber that truth is not subjective, that facts are facts and lies are lies, I know that she believes Grandma Nellie.

"You've never told me how you did it, how you survived it all," Ted said, trying to pry out some detail in defense of the story he so wanted to believe.

"The bear... the bear got me through it," Grandma Nellie replied.

Nellie

Some things are worse than losing your family. My daddy, my stepmother, my brother—they were all dead, and all I had left was Teddy. No matter what they would do to me, no matter where they would take me, I wasn't going without Teddy.

The neighbor lady thought I wasn't well-behaved, so she wouldn't keep me. They should have. I would have been good, would have done whatever she wanted, as soon as I learned. But she didn't give me time. Her daughter was having nightmares because of what happened to my family, so she decided to take me to the orphanage.

It took a long time to get there. We drove along winding roads, past fields, ponds, and forests. Teddy and I pressed our noses against the window and tried not to think too much about what was happening to us.

The orphanage. Gore Orphanage. We were orphans now.

Those look-alike girls were laughing at us when we finally came to the place. I don't know why. They were orphans, too. Teddy doesn't like it when people laugh at us, and neither do I.

The woman who opened the door was scary and she was wearing a dead furry thing around her neck. The people at the orphanage liked dead things. She wore them a lot, and there were also stuffed ones all around as decorations. The fox in the hallway looked like it was

29

still alive, like it was trying to run away, but it was trapped, just like us.

When Mrs. Pryor made me leave her office to talk to the neighbor lady, I listened at the door. They were talking about money.

That's when I first saw Ernst. He was a very tall man, dressed in overalls, and was mopping the floor and whistling. There was something not right about his whistle. I don't know what it was, but it made Teddy and me nervous.

Bill Townsend as Ernst

As soon as the neighbor lady left, Mrs. Pryor stopped smiling. She grabbed me hard.

"Now, it is time for you to learn to behave," she said, as she dragged me upstairs.

Esther and Miss Lillian were nice to us, but nearly everyone in the orphanage was mean. I don't know why Esther liked Ernst. He came into our room at night when everybody is sleeping. I saw him and I heard him whistling.

That mean girl, Anna, liked Ernst, too. She told me that he kills all of the meat for the orphanage. I don't know what kind of animals he traps, but the meat is better than the mush, once you get used to it. He tried to touch me one day when we were having dinner. We were just sitting at the table, and he came around with his mop and bucket and touched my arm.

Anna's hair was curly, like mine, but pale blonde. She wore it in a thick braid tied with a cream bow and she never took off her necklace, a strange-looking silver and blue cross. Anna was particular about how she looked, even though her dress was torn in spots. I suppose she looked pretty, but she was a mean girl and that made her ugly.

When I burned my hand with the hot iron on the first day of work, she smiled. Then Mrs. Pryor blew cigarette smoke into my face and took my bear away. Miss Lillian shouldn't have let either of them do that to me, but Miss Lillian is timid. She got Teddy back, but she should never have allowed him to be taken. That made Teddy and me both very angry.

Nobody had nightclothes at Gore Orphanage. We just took off our shoes and climbed into bed. Most of the time, they locked the bedroom door when we go to sleep. I know, because I get up in the night a lot. One night, not long after I came there, they forgot.

It was dark in the hallway, and strange shadows fell everywhere. My bear and I went down the narrow stairs from the attic slowly, carefully, quietly. Somebody was moving around below, and I thought I heard whistling, but this was our only chance. We had to get out.

Quietly, carefully—down to the second floor. We looked over the railing, but I couldn't see anyone downstairs. A stair creaked, and we froze for a moment. The shadows of the trees outside moved across the wall. Just a little further, and we would be free. I pictured it in my mind. Just down the last few stairs, out the door, and into the woods, then run and never stop.

Someone was downstairs. I was sure I saw something moving out of the corner of my eye as we turned the bend in the stairs, but Teddy said to keep going. I ran to the front door, but it wouldn't open. I tugged as hard as I could. It was all that was left before we could run, but I couldn't open it. There was no way out.

I sat at the door, crying and holding bear, when the door at the other end of the hall began to creak open. I knew who lived down there. It was Ernst, and he was coming to get me. I just knew it.

The door opened a little further, and a figure was silhouetted against the light. I couldn't see the face, but it wasn't him. Instead, a little blonde girl came out from the basement and over to me. She came closer and closer, then knelt beside us.

"It's time for bed," she said, and took me by the hand to go upstairs. I had no choice, but I wouldn't give up. My bear and I were going to get out. Somehow, someway, we would leave that place.

That girl, Irene, wasn't the only one I saw going in and out of the basement. Another day, as we were all coming inside, I saw Anna go over to him and the two of them disappeared down the basement door. She didn't come back before bedtime, so I had to ask Esther about her when we were lying in bed.

"Is Anna safe?"

Esther looked at me as if I had just asked her the stupidest question, but it wasn't stupid. I know.

"Yes... Ernie and her are just playing."

"Playing what?"

"Ernie likes to play with all the little girls," Esther told me.

"Do you play with him?"

"Ernie gives me cookies when we play," she said, with a great big smile. I don't like cookies that much.

Anna was back the next morning, but she didn't get up for bed inspection. She didn't move at all, even when Mrs. Pryor came over. Irene started crying.

"Ernst! Ernst!" screamed Mrs. Pryor, and we all heard him come running up the stairs. He stopped when he saw Anna just lying there.

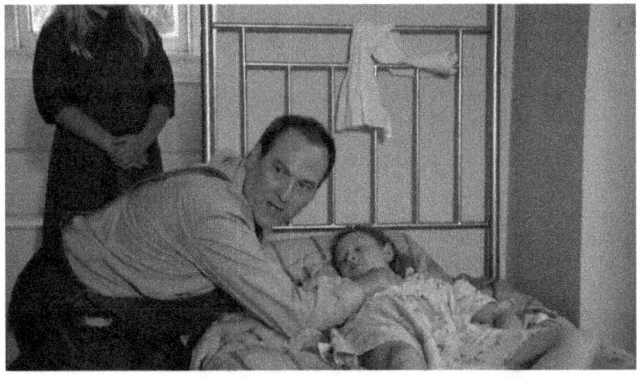

"Look, just look at her!" Mrs. Pryor screamed. Ernst walked towards the bed, then knelt and tried to wake her. He was sobbing and calling her name, but it didn't matter. Anna was dead.

"Clean up this mess… clean it up or so help me God…" Mrs. Pryor was glaring at Ernst, who called for Harmon. He'd been standing there, right at the edge of the girl's side of the room, watching.

Ernst and Harmon lifted her limp body out of the bed. Her arms hung down and her pale hands flopped as they carried her away. We heard their footsteps shuffle out of the room, down the yellow stairs, down, down, and away. Mrs. Pryor followed them out, her brow furrowed and her hands clenched.

Miss Lillian came upstairs just afterwards and told us to go outside and play. She took me by the hand and led me out of the bedroom. When we went outside, the other girls were sitting in the grass. Irene was still crying, and now some of the other girls were, too. Miss Lillian and I sat down on the steps. Her hands were shaking as she opened up her purse and pulled out a cigarette case. She lit one. I'd never seen her smoke before.

Emma Smith as Nellie and Keri Maletto as Miss Lillian

'We're all going to miss Anna," she told me. Maybe Irene would miss her, but Esther and I wouldn't be teased any more, and neither would Miss Lillian. Anna was a nasty, mean girl, and everyone has to die sometime.

"Everyone dies…" I told Miss Lillian.

"Everyone here has seen the face of death," she said, taking another puff of her cigarette, "But I won't die any time soon."

I looked over at the little girls in the grass. Some of them were crying, and other ones were hugging them.

"I should be crying, like the others," I told Miss Lillian. I couldn't cry. I didn't have any tears. I had barely met Anna, she was mean to me, and now she was dead. So were my brother, my father, my stepmother.

"We all handle loss differently," Miss Lillian told me, putting her arm around my shoulders, "You're a special little girl and don't let anyone tell you differently."

Miss Lillian and I sat there together, her arm around me, for a long time, watching the wind in the trees. We didn't talk anymore, but I could tell Miss Lillian liked me. She cared about me so much that she sat with me, not with the girls who were crying.

We were outside for most of the day, until it was time to eat. Miss Lillian called us all together and we walked into the house, past Ernst, who was mopping up the floor in the downstairs hallway again. I noticed that Miss Lillian wouldn't look at him as we walked by. Each of the children behind her followed her example. They turned their heads away, but I didn't, and I saw that Ernst was very sad.

When we went into the dining room, I sat down beside Esther. There was already bread on the table, and I was so hungry that I grabbed a roll and hid it in my lap right away. Everyone would be starving, and we weren't supposed to eat until Mrs. Pryor read from the Bible, but I knew the big boys would take all the bread before I could get any if I waited.

"I'm scared," Esther told me softly.

"Things will get better now," I told her. Anna would never call her a pester again, would never sing to Miss Lillian about influenza.

"But Anna?" Buddy asked.

"Shh… be quiet!" Esther warned him. There were too many people listening. I sometimes think Buddy isn't very bright. He should have figured things out.

"Buddy, think about it," I whispered. I could see the wheels turning in his mind and he looked across the table at the big boys.

"Harmon?" he asked.

"No," I told him, but he only looked more confused.

"Why would Ernst…" Buddy began, and I had to shush him before he said any more.

"But what will we do?" Esther asked. I think she understood, at least.

"Nothing," I told her.

The door opened and Mrs. Pryor walked in, followed by Miss Lillian and Ernst. Mrs. Pryor had the Bible, but she didn't read to us.

"Children, Anna has left us," she said. "Though I know you would like to pay your last respects, we have decided that it would not be appropriate."

"We did?" Miss Lillian retorted.

Mrs. Pryor shot her a nasty look, then continued.

"This incident has already been upsetting enough for the children and this institution, but we must not allow another day to be wasted. Is that not correct, Miss Lillian?"

Miss Lillian looked upset, but she put her head down and murmured, "yes."

"Good," continued Mrs. Pryor. "Now we can assure you that no more accidents like the one that befell poor Anna will happen again. Is that not correct, Ernst?"

He wouldn't meet her eyes either, and looked like he was about to cry.

"Ja, sure," he said.

Mrs. Pryor wasn't done yet.

"As a tribute to Anna, there will be no dinner tonight."

Buddy looked at the bread on the table, then at me, his eyes wide. I could almost hear his stomach rumbling.

"No dinner! I'm going to be a starvin' marvin!" he said.

"Look here," I whispered, and showed him the roll hidden in my lap. He was my friend.

We went straight to bed and Miss Lillian locked us in, all except Harmon. He had stayed behind after dinner and I saw him talking to Ernst.

There was a little hole in the door, probably from an older lock. Esther, Buddy, and I tried to look through it into the hallway, but we couldn't see anything.

"We're trapped!" Esther said.

"We need to know what's going on with Anna," I told them.

"But you said we should do nothing," Esther replied. She looked a little annoyed.

"That was to shut both of you up," I told her. Something strange was going on, and we needed to find out what it was. I could hear an odd noise outside. We all climbed up on top of the window seat in one of the dormer windows and looked down at the yard at the side of the house.

We could just barely see two figures through the branches of the tree. Ernst and Harmon were digging a hole. The noise I'd noticed was the sound of their shovels cutting into the ground. Something was lying on the grass, something pale gold and green. It looked like Anna.

On one of the nights when I couldn't sleep, I had discovered something amazing in the bathroom. I needed it now, and I needed Buddy and Esther to help me. I had to trust them. I gave Buddy part of the bread I had in my pocket, then led them both to the bathroom. Nobody noticed us all going in together, or maybe they just didn't care. I closed the door and locked it, then opened the towel closet to show Esther and Buddy what I had discovered. One of the boards at the side of the wall was loose, and you could climb right through into another closet on the other side.

"Yuck!" said Esther, wrinkling up her face. There were probably lots of spiders in there, and Esther hated anything creepy crawly.

"Quit being a scaredy cat," I told her. I needed both of them to come with me. It would be an adventure.

I took my lantern and matches out from behind the towels. I wasn't very good with the matches and it took a couple of tries to light one and then light the candle, but soon it was casting an orange glow.

"Come on," I whispered, and we all climbed through the side of the towel closet and into a clothing closet in the back hallway, right above the stairs. "We have to be very quiet, understand?" I told them before opening the door, and they nodded solemnly. Then I opened the door slowly and peeked into the hall. It was all clear, so I motioned for them to follow and we crept down the back stairs. We could hear Mrs. Pryor's voice, indistinctly at first, but clearer and clearer as we got closer. I put my ear up to the hallway door and the others copied me.

"The matter is settled," she said, "I do not foresee him having any more incidents."

"What's she talking about?" Buddy whispered. Esther and I stared at him.

"Ernst," she said. At least Esther understood.

"I do not pay you to think, only to solve problems as they arise," Mrs. Pryor continued angrily. Then I heard her hang up the phone and footsteps outside the door. Carefully, slowly, I opened it just a crack and we looked out.

Mrs. Pryor, Ernst, and Harmon were all standing by the stuffed fox and the big fireplace. They didn't see us.

"The little difficulty is resolved," Mrs. Pryor said, and Ernst nodded. "Just hold up your side of the bargain."

"Ja, Frau Pryor," he said, and Harmon held out something small which spun and glittered in the light as he offered it to her. It was the funny-shaped cross necklace Anna always wore. She told me once that it was a special Russian cross that was supposed to protect her. Guess it hadn't worked.

Mrs. Pryor took the necklace, then turned to go upstairs. So did we. We had to get back to bed before she noticed we were missing. We raced up the back stairs, into the clothes closet, squeezed through the side between the boards, and were back in the bathroom. Esther and Buddy went straight back to bed, but I had to put the lantern away where nobody would find it. My pretty white dress was all covered in dust. I was still trying to clean it off when I heard the key turn in the lock and footsteps in the bedroom.

"Where's Nellie?" I heard Mrs. Pryor ask.

"The bathroom," Esther responded, and the footsteps grew closer.

"Child, come out of there immediately."

I opened the door slowly.

"I'm sorry, Mrs. Pryor," I said sweetly, "I was just cleaning up."

She sent Teddy and me straight to bed without even noticing the dirt on my dress. Esther smiled at me as I climbed under the sheets.

"Good night, Nellie," she whispered, "I'm so glad you're here."

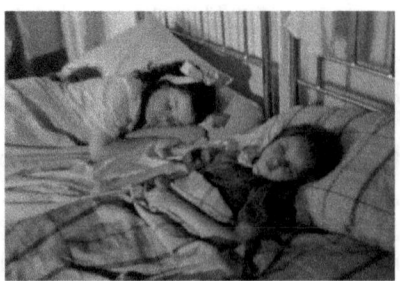

Emma Smith as Nellie and Nora Hoyle as Esther

40

The next morning, at breakfast, Buddy was all smiles.

"Last night was fun!" he said, as soon as I sat down beside him. How could he be so stupid?

"Buddy, you have to keep it a secret," I whispered angrily.

He looked confused. "Why?"

"Because no one can know what we did."

"I can't tell anyone?"

I never should have trusted him.

"No!" I replied, and I was so angry that I forgot to whisper.

Miss Lillian came striding in, wearing a new black and red dress and a jaunty little hat. She looked so much happier, and so much prettier, than usual that I knew even before she started to talk that something special must be happening.

"Children, I have great news," she announced. "Schoolboy Rowe from the Detroit Tigers will be here today." Both Buddy and Esther perked up.

"Who's that?" I asked them.

"My favorite pitcher," Buddy replied, "I got his baseball card."

He had a whole stack of baseball cards hiding behind that pipe, and most of them were Detroit. I didn't remember this Schoolboy character, though.

"He's a dreamboat. His wife Edna is so lucky," Esther added.

Neither of them noticed that Harmon and his friends were listening to us. Harmon leaned in and whispered something to the blond boy with the overalls, who nodded. The one in the sweater smiled at us.

Buddy sprung up from his chair and rushed away.

"Miss Lillian… Miss Lillian, is he really coming?"

She bent towards him. "Would I lie to you?"

"I'm just so excited. Yesterday, and now this. It's so much fun!" Miss Lillian looked at him, concerned. She had no idea what he was talking about, and things needed to stay that way, but Buddy just wouldn't shut up.

"There was nothing fun about yesterday, Buddy. Anna is gone," Miss Lillian said sadly.

"I know," Buddy responded, smiling. "We seen them bury Anna in the back yard."

Esther rushed forward as soon as she heard what he was saying. Miss Lillian looked aghast.

"You mustn't tell such tall tales!"

"Yes," Esther echoed, "you should not tell such tall tales."

How could he have done that? Was he really that dumb or did he want us to get in trouble? Esther was smart. She knew we had to keep what we'd seen a secret, but Buddy… I should never have trusted him. I would never trust him like that again.

"Can I be excused, Miss Lillian?" I asked, and she agreed. I breathed a sigh of relief, but then she said that she wanted to talk with Buddy and Esther a little longer. There was nothing I could do except to leave them there with her. I could only hope that Esther would keep Buddy from squealing on what we'd done.

Mrs. Pryor

When I was a little girl, Daddy made certain that Frank and I knew that the place of children was to be seen and not heard. We were well-bred little children, who knew our place, knew which forks to use and how to stand beside our chairs and ask to be excused from the table. I had ponies and painting lessons, French governesses and immense dolls' houses with real china and silver. My frocks were made for me of Brussels lace and the finest silks. When we were older, we went to the continent every summer to see great works of art.

People say that Daddy spoiled us, but no matter what he gave us, it couldn't make up for the loss of our mother. She had never really recovered from Frank's birth and died when he was less than a year old. Most of my memories are of her lying in bed in a lacy nightgown, pale and weak. Every morning, as soon as I woke up, I would run into her room.

"Don't leap on the bed, Victoria," the doctor had said, "You'll injure her."

I would climb up carefully, throwing my arms around her neck, and she would kiss me. Years later, one of the governesses had told Daddy that I was "not a loveable child," but my mother had loved me. One morning, I ran into her room and the bed was empty.

Daddy chose Captain John Pryor for me to marry. Neither John nor I had any say in the matter, but the People Who Mattered told me I was lucky to have such a catch. They knew he was marrying me for the money. Daddy gave me to him as a prize, a just reward, but the baby died and John died in the Great War. Frank was grown up and gone, and only Daddy and I were at home. He gave me everything I could want, everything except his love. That was reserved for the orphans.

Daddy loved orphans, especially the girls. I wanted Daddy to love me, too, but he never could. I was always last, after those little trollops, after Frank, even though I was older, because he was the son and heir.

Lillian Laszlo was dressed to the nines, or at least as far as her modest means would take her, when the baseball player came, in a too-tight black and red dress and a hat which she had bedecked in beads and embroidery. Its gaudy folk style betrayed her peasant origins, but doubtless she thought it very flattering. Lillian had the advantage of youth, but I was wearing a remarkable silk dress which the famous Mr. Rowe could not help but notice. The orphan girls had made it to my specifications, with sleeves like those Joan Crawford wore in *Letty Lynton* as the beautiful socialite who accidentally poisons her lover while she is attempting to commit suicide. It was a marvelous film, and Joan Crawford's wardrobe was simply divine. I ought to go to the movies more often. I need some distraction from the banality of my existence. Her dress was white, but mine was made from iridescent tongues of flame silk taffeta in just the right shade to compliment my autumnal hair and complexion and trimmed in deep brown and bright canary yellow. My hat was tilted mischievously.

We watched him walk towards the front door, and he was every bit as handsome as he looked in the papers—tall and shapely, wearing an impeccably tailored suit in place of his baseball uniform. He was young, probably not even thirty, and with an easy bearing.

Keri Maletto as Miss Lillian and Nick LaMantia as Schoolboy Rowe

"Mr. Rowe," I said, "Welcome to Gore Orphanage." His true name, I had learned, was not that puerile "Schoolboy," but rather the much more dignified "Lynwood." It suited him, although his wide grin was that of a boy.

"Mrs. Pryor, I presume," he responded in that southern American drawl which I had found so charming ever since I had come here as a girl. He bent over my hand and kissed it, true gentleman that he was, looking up at me with eyes that would melt a heart of stone. His large hand enveloped and caressed mine. Then he turned to the fidgeting figure he had not deigned to notice previously.

"And you are Miss Lillian," he said, kissing her hand as well. He lingered over it even longer than he had mine. "Thank you for inviting me."

Lillian had made the suggestion, but I had invited him. Nothing happens at Gore Orphanage without my fiat. I had allowed her to contact him, since she had somehow previously made his acquaintance. How the dirt-poor daughter of a Hungarian butcher had met the matinee idol of baseball I will never know, but it does call into question her professional conduct.

"Anything for the children," Lillian chirped vapidly.

I drew him forward, leaving Lillian behind us. The children, boys and girls, had been gathered in the girls' workroom. It was the largest presentable room in the orphanage, and we must keep up appearances.

Lynwood Rowe looked about the foyer curiously, taking in the grand staircase, the print of Andersonville above the fireplace, and the elegant Roman dividing columns. He cast his eye admiringly on the statue of Don Quixote and Ernst's taxidermy fox. I ought to have had Ernst paint the ceiling.

"Tell me about this place," he drawled.

"My father was an orphan himself," I replied, looking full into his warm dark eyes, "so it would seem understandable he would spend so much on the children."

"Good man, your father," he said, bathing me in his radiant smile. He had no idea, none whatsoever, about what sort of man my father had really been. Few people do.

"You might say that…" I responded, a trifle wryly. "This way, Mr. Rowe." Mae, the little red-haired girl, was standing in the door watching him intently. She is man-crazy already, that one. I must speak to Lillian about keeping close eye on her.

The orphans sprung to attention as we entered the room. At least they were showing Mr. Rowe that they had manners despite their lack of proper breeding.

"What do we say to Mr. Rowe, children?" I prompted.

"Thank you, Mr. Rowe," they chorused in their abrasive, high-pitched voices.

"My pleasure," Lynwood Rowe replied, in a voice as smooth and sweet as southern molasses. Lillian brought a few of the older girls forward.

"Can you say it, please?" I found myself asking, as girlish as they, "for the children's sake?"

When Rowe had first leapt to prominence by setting a record for consecutive winning games, he had been unprepared for the limelight and, in the midst of a radio interview, had asked his fiancée "How'm I doing, Edna?" The poor man had never been allowed to forget his gaffe, and those words had become inexorably linked to him. Still, I had to hear them from his very mouth.

He looked a bit bashful, but obliged.

"How'm I doing, Edna?"

The girls looked to each other and swooned. I tried to retain my composure.

"I'm guessing it would be good if I spent some time with the young uns," he added, crouching down. "Gather round," he said, beckoning the children close. "You all eating your vittles?" he asked.

Most of them nodded obediently, but I saw a few shake their heads "no." I made a mental note of which of the little guttersnipes would need to be corrected.

The little Italian boy, the one they called Buddy, sprung up and raced towards Mr. Rowe.

"Will you sign my baseball card?" he asked. I had no idea that the child had somehow retained personal property.

"Sure, kid," replied the ever-obliging baseball player, and Buddy ran out of the room. I heard his little feet pounding up the stairs. There was a pause, a thud, and then he raced back down and into the room, hurtling his little body at Harmon who, unprepared, was knocked to the floor.

"You took my card!" he screamed, pummeling Harmon with his tiny fists. Schoolboy Rowe smiled at the sight of the boys fighting, and I knew just what I had to do to please him.

"You two want to fight? Then fight!" I told the boys. We would give Mr. Rowe blood sport for his entertainment. The boys began to tussle on the floor. Harmon was twice Buddy's age and much stronger, but the little man was filled with rage.

"Hit him!" I instructed. Mr. Rowe's smile had faded.

Harmon obligingly began to punch Buddy, looking up at me uncertainly.

"Harder!"

Harmon paused in doubt, then turned back to Buddy and began to wallop him.

"Give it up, squirt," Harmon said. He had pinned Buddy to the floor.

"Never," the boy replied. "You took my card."

"I didn't take it, you little rat!"

Lynwood Rowe turned to Lillian and said something, then the two of them began to walk out of the room. He was leaving, and with her. He had only just come and he was going, never to return. I had hardly had a moment with him, and the orphans had driven him away. I gave them everything, all I had, and they had taken everything from me. My father, a man of immense wealth and little kindness, had left the bulk of his estate in a trust for these brats and, in his largesse, bound me to dispense charity to the ungrateful wretches. Instead of living in comfort, as would befit my station as the widow of the hero pilot Captain Pryor and the only daughter of Francis Gore, I was trapped in a decaying mansion with a pack of prepubescent human vermin.

"Enough! Stand up!" I screamed. "This is how you repay my kindness? You disgust me. Little mongrels, money munchers, gnawing away at my inheritance—and for what? You will never amount to anything. You are nothing! Nothing! No one loves you… no one…"

They stared at me blankly.

"Say it!" I prompted, "Say it!" I stomped my foot. "No one loves you, no one wants you."

They began to mutter it. "No one loves us, no one wants us."

"Louder!"

They would obey me and they would remember who they were. They were all scum, vermin, parasites. They would be grateful for all I had given them. They merited none of it.

"No one loves us, no one wants us."

"Again!" I began to conduct them. They would say it properly, in rhythm.

"No one loves us, no one wants us. No one loves us, no one wants us."

They need a reminder from time to time, least they forget their place in the world.

I chose the reading for their evening prayer with especial care that night. It is my duty to mold them spiritually, also. The two boys who had caused all the ruckus, Buddy and Harmon, would sit at table, but with empty plates before them. They would not be given anything to eat for breakfast, either. Not only would this remind them that they are dependent on my charity for their very existence, but it would also save a few cents in the bargain. I have learned to be frugal out of necessity. I opened the Bible.

"But the fearful, and unbelieving, and abominable, and murderers, and whoremongers, and sorcerers, and idolaters, and all liars," I gave especial emphasis to this phrase, "shall have their part in the lake which burneth with fire and brimstone."

"Amen," chorused the children. Forever and ever, amen and amen.

Daddy loved orphans. He loved them more than me.

Evan Mitchell, Skye Durst, Cienna Cetera, John Kaminsky, McKenna Hewitt, Mikey Voytovich, Sabastian Synuria, Arria Mitchell, and Nicolette and Mackenzie Cloutier as orphans with Emma Smith as Nellie.

IV.

Ted

When we were told that Grandma Nellie was being released from the rehabilitation center, my daughter Amber could barely contain her excitement. She had made miles of garland from strips of colored construction paper and draped them all over her room and created a giant banner using butcher paper. "WELCOM HOME!" it had originally read, until Sarah told her that she'd spelled it wrong. Now, a tiny" e" had been squeezed in: "WELCOMeHOME!" She'd also drawn the bear on the banner.

"He'll be so happy that she's home again," Amber told me, hugging the bear. "We both missed Grandma Nellie very much."

Amber wanted to take the day off from school to bring Grandma Nellie home, but Sarah wouldn't hear of it. She was resentful of Grandma Nellie's growing role in Amber's life. I think she somehow felt it took away from her own, but a child can never have too much love. It was good for Grandma Nellie, too. She had been starved of love for so many years, especially when she was Amber's age. It was almost as if she was able to put the traumas of her past to rest by giving Amber the safe and happy childhood she had been denied.

I called Mom to give her an update on Grandma Nellie. As usual, she wanted to talk about everything else.

"When are you coming to see me?" she asked. "I want to see my little girl."

I promised her we would all come out soon. We both knew, though neither of us said it, that "we" included Grandma Nellie. They hadn't seen each other in who knows how many years, and there was bound to be some friction, but Grandma Nellie was well into her eighties now and it might be the last chance they would have. The fall had scared me. I hated to imagine losing Grandma Nellie without trying, yet again, to patch the relationship between my mother and my grandmother.

Obviously, I wasn't there when Mom was a little girl. I don't know exactly what happened, but life was tough, and Mom holds a lot of resentment. What I do know for certain is that Grandma Nellie, like so many parents, tried to do her best for her daughter. That's all any of us can do for our children. Sarah is much younger than I, and still believes somehow that she can give Amber a perfect life—a childhood better than her own. But childhood is always bittersweet, full of crystalline moments of simple joy and the deep hurts that we somehow remember forever.

It means a lot to me for us to be together—to be a family. We are not one of those families which has yearly reunions in park pavilions. The five of us could have a family reunion in a booth at a restaurant, but we don't. We haven't all been together since before Amber was born.

As soon as Grandma Nellie is up to it, I'll pack them all in the car and we'll go see Mom. I'll let Amber do all the talking. If anyone can overcome all the years of bitterness and mistrust, it is my little ray of sunshine.

There's the small complication of Grandma Nellie's former roommate, the one who died. Apparently, her autopsy suggested that her death could very well have been caused by neglect or abuse in the facility, and the family is suing. Grandma Nellie is the only neutral party who could have witnessed anything, so they want her to testify. Her mind is sound for a woman of her age, but she's insisted again and again that she never saw anything, that Stella just didn't wake up one morning.

"They weren't the most attentive people, but honestly, Theodore, it was hard for anyone to tell if that woman was alive or dead half the time, except for the coughing. I did notice she wasn't coughing, but it was such a blasted relief that I fell asleep as soon as it was quiet. I woke up when they were carting her away."

I wonder if it's true, or if she just doesn't want me to know how bad things were there. We all hear stories of nursing home abuse, of bad eldercare facilities and disinterested or malicious workers. Being in the healthcare field myself, I know that all too many of them, tragically, are true. When I worked in behavioral health, I saw things that disgusted and angered me. I was young and afraid to speak out against my coworkers, but I left that job as soon as I could. The elderly, the mentally ill, the developmentally disabled—they are all potential victims because they cannot speak out for themselves or no one believes them when they do. When the days are long, the staff is small, and the pay is low, it becomes alarmingly easy for caretakers to overlook the humanity of those in their charge. I had done my research and believed that Grandma Nellie's rehab center was one of the better ones, but you never can really know unless you are there every moment—and if you could be, your loved ones wouldn't be in a facility to begin with.

Grandma Nellie is very stubborn and very independent. I didn't see any bruises or bedsores, but she doesn't like us to help her bathe or dress. Institutions never sit well with Grandma Nellie, probably because of the orphanage. Whatever they did to poor Stella, it wouldn't have phased Grandma Nellie much. Somehow, she probably expected it.

Esther

Harmon is dangerous. He must have seen where Buddy hid his cards. Nobody else knew, except Buddy's best friends. It was a secret, a cross your heart and hope to die secret. Buddy said he wasn't scared of Harmon, that he didn't care if Harmon beat him up again. Buddy's daddy gave him those cards and they were all he had left.

We were all sitting at dinner that night, except that Buddy wasn't allowed to eat and neither was Harmon. The older boys were staring at poor Buddy like they wanted to smash his face in and Harmon kept looking over and drawing his fingers across his neck like he was going to kill us. I felt bad about eating in front of Buddy, but I was so hungry that I finally just had to. Buddy was my best friend before Nellie came, and now we are all best friends together. We have secrets that nobody else knows.

We know what happened to Anna, that Ernie and Harmon buried her in the yard. When we are allowed to go out in the yard, I watch the boys play tag right over where they put her, but I won't walk on her grave. I tried to tell Ralph that he shouldn't go over there, but I couldn't tell him why, so he just shrugged his shoulders and went back to playing.

Nellie got really mad at us when Buddy almost spilled the beans to Miss Lillian. I had to try to patch things up and told Miss Lillian that he was just making it up. I think she wanted to believe me. She probably doesn't know what happened to Anna. She did go talk to Mrs. Pryor after she talked to us, though. I hope Buddy doesn't get into more trouble.

I like having secrets with Buddy and Nellie, even if what we know makes me sad sometimes. There was a little boy who died of a seizure when I first got here. His name was Harry. I wonder sometimes if he is buried in the yard, like Anna. I wonder how many children are out there, how many times Ernie has dug up the yard in the night.

Next time I play with Ernie, I might ask him. Then again, I might not. It would probably make him sad. Ernie loves children, and Anna was one of his favorites. He plays lots of games with us girls, like the walnut game, and the cookie game, and piggyback rides. Last time we played the walnut game, he let me go first.

"Esther, Esther," all the girls called out, but I gave the walnut to Irene because she was still sad about Anna. Ernie is very particular about how we play the walnut game and he gets upset if we don't follow the rules.

I told Nellie that we needed to keep an eye on Buddy, but we couldn't do anything to protect him when Harmon stopped him on the way to the bathroom.

"Enjoy your last night on earth, little man," Harmon said, but Buddy wouldn't just let it go. He gritted his jaw and held up a clenched fist.

"I ain't afraid of you, Harmon!" he said, but Harmon just laughed.

"Go ahead, hit me. Hit me if you dare." Buddy tried to swing, but Harmon put his big hand on Buddy's head and held him back.

"Try again!"

Poor Buddy swung and swung, but his arms weren't long enough and Harmon was too big and strong. Harmon's friends were leaning against the dormer, watching and snickering.

"I'll get you, Harmon!" Buddy said, but Harmon just gave him a shove and Buddy fell.

"You'll never be a man, squirt," Harmon said, as he turned towards the bathroom. Buddy was crying, and I ran to him. I didn't see Nellie streak past until she had already hit Harmon right where it hurts boys the most. He bent over, and she bit his ear. Harmon screamed, but Nellie didn't care. There was blood on her mouth when she looked up.

Alerted by the scream, Mrs. Pryor came striding into the room. Nellie and Harmon sprung up from the floor.

"What is going on here?" she asked.

"She bit me," Harmon replied, showing her his bloody ear.

"Why would you bite him?" Mrs. Pryor asked Nellie, "Who started this mess?"

Nellie looked at Buddy and me, but we just couldn't say anything. I know Nellie was just trying to protect Buddy, but she shouldn't have bit Harmon. We knew that nothing we could say would save her. Mrs. Pryor never believes girls against boys.

"Well then, Miss Nellie," Mrs. Pryor continued, "You will need some correction. You must learn that pain will be received as quickly as it is inflicted here." Mrs. Pryor grabbed Nellie by the arm and dragged her out. Nellie looked back at us, pleading, but there was nothing we could do. I held Buddy tight and he just kept crying.

Thump, thump, thump. I don't know what Mrs. Pryor was doing to Nellie out on the steps, but it sounded terrible. It sounded like she was dragging her down, and Nellie was hitting every step. Thump, thump, thump. Buddy flinched with each thud.

David Ziglear as an orphan and Brandon Mangin, Jr. as Buddy

There was a long pause, and then we heard Nellie screaming. Harmon grinned.

"What do you think it is?" he asked the big blond boy, Mikey.

"The ruler?"

"Nah," the other big boy, Abe, replied. "Probably the spoon. She loves to whack little girl's bottoms with that one."

The boys all laughed.

When Nellie came back into the room, she didn't have her bear anymore and she could barely walk, but she went right past Harmon and his friends with her chin held high.

"Did you enjoy your whipping?" Harmon asked.

Buddy walked towards her, his lower lip trembling.

"I'm sorry, Nellie."

"So am I," I said.

"Crying baby Buddy," Harmon taunted from his bed, "You deserve better friends that these two. Night, losers." He stretched out in bed and pulled up his sheet.

Nellie reached out to Buddy. Her eyes were solemn. She had taken a beating because she protected him. We were best friends.

"Buddy," she said, "You will never have to cry again. I promise."

Buddy smiled through his tears. Nellie is taller and stronger than either one of us, and he had just seen that she would protect him.

"I'm so happy you're our friend," I told her as we walked back to the girls' side of the room. We took off our shoes and climbed into bed. Nellie turned on her side and hugged the pillow in place of her bear.

"Good night, Nellie," I whispered, but she was already asleep.

I woke up before it was time to get out of bed. Downstairs, I could hear Mrs. Pryor playing the piano. She isn't very good, but she plays all the time. Suddenly, she stopped, and I could hear yelling. I looked over at Nellie, but she was still asleep, her dark curly hair spread over her pillow.

We heard footsteps coming up the stairs, louder and louder, then the door flew open. Mrs. Pryor was in the boys' side of the room, and she was screaming "Monster, monster!"

"What'd I do?" I heard Harmon say, between Mrs. Pryor's screams and the sound of hitting.

"You know what you did, murderer," she responded, and I sat up in bed. Did Harmon kill Anna? Had he killed again? But who? There was only one person I could think of whom Harmon had threatened. I remembered his words from the night before—"enjoy your last night on earth, little man." It couldn't be…

She hit him again and again. Nellie was awake now, and listening.

"He was just a little boy!"

Harmon started crying out in Polish. His mother was Polish, although he was named after his daddy, and Harmon mostly spoke Polish before he came to the orphanage because his daddy wasn't there to teach him English. I couldn't tell what he was saying, but he sounded really upset.

Jeremy Kaluza as Harmon

"You'll never harm anyone again," I heard Mrs. Pryor say, and then there was a dragging sound, and the thump, thump, thump, on the stairs again.

Nellie and I were both sitting up.

"Did she say murderer?" I asked, "Is Buddy…"

"Yes," Nellie said slowly. "Buddy is dead."

I started to cry and Nellie held me and stroked my hair.

"He was our Buddy," I said. We were best friends together. We had secrets that nobody else knew.

59

"I know," Nellie said softly.

We never saw Harmon again, and we never found out what they did with Buddy's body. I looked in the yard next to where we saw them bury Anna, but it didn't look like anything had changed. I found a few smooth, round rocks and piled them up, then tucked wildflowers into the cracks. I would always remember our Buddy.

That's when the nightmares began. As soon as I fell asleep, I dreamt that someone was trying to kill me during the night, just like Anna and Buddy. Hands were reaching out and holding me down, but I could never see who it was. I woke up screaming.

Ernie came running into the room. I could hear his big, heavy shoes on the floor and knew he was coming for me even before I saw him.

"Be peaceful, be peaceful, my little Schätzlein," Ernie said, kneeling beside my bed. He stroked my hair. "Gut... very gut. You calm, ja?"

"Someone's trying to kill me," I told him, and his forehead wrinkled.

"No one will kill my little Schätzlein, no one," he promised, his blue eyes troubled.

"You'll protect me?"

"Ja," he said, "Now you sleep."

He tucked my sheet around me with his great big hands. His fingernails are always a little dirty, but I don't mind.

"Eyes closed, sleep," he told me, and began to sing softly. It's a little song from his country, he told me once, but he doesn't remember all the words. Ernie doesn't remember a lot of things because he was gassed in the war. "Schlaf, Kindlein, schlaf," he sang, and I began to drift back into sleep. The last thing I remembered was the gentle brush of his goodnight kiss.

The next morning, Miss Lillian woke us up.

"Where's Mrs. Pryor?" somebody asked her.

"Mrs. Pryor is… going about her business," she told us, and we all began to smile.

With Mrs. Pryor and Harmon gone, it was like a fog had lifted in the orphanage. Every room seemed sunnier, and none of us could believe what we saw when we went down for breakfast—bacon and eggs for everyone.

Miss Lillian read from the Bible, but it didn't sound anything like what Mrs. Pryor usually reads us.

"And whosoever shall offend one of these little ones that believe in me, it is better for him that a millstone were hanged about his neck, and he were cast into the sea. Amen." I wondered if that was what had happened to Harmon. I imagined Mrs. Pryor throwing him into the lake with a great big rock tied to him. She was standing on a rowboat and shouting, "Murderer, murderer!" Harmon was protesting in Polish, but then he was underwater and bubbles were coming out of his mouth instead of words.

"Amen," we all said, and dug into the bacon and eggs. Everything seemed less real than the nightmares I'd had, especially when Ernie came in and gave us each candy. There was saltwater taffy, and hard tack, and all sorts of sweets, each one wrapped in its own paper.

Instead of morning work detail, Miss Lillian and Ernie took us all straight outside. Ernie gave me extra candy that he'd hidden in the pockets of his overalls. Miss Lillian had given Nellie her bear back after Mrs. Pryor took it during the beating, but Nellie left Bear with Miss Lillian while we played. She almost never lets him go.

I ran over to Ernie and got him to play with us, then Nellie and I went back for Miss Lillian. We all spun around until we were dizzy and the adults laughed just like they were children, just like everything that had happened had only been a bad dream.

Foreground: Skye Durst and McKenna Hewitt as orphans

Ernie took the boys fishing and they caught us dinner, which was served up with heaping bowls of mashed potatoes. Miss Lillian read us a story about an orphan girl named Anne who got taken in by old people on a farm. It was a good story, but nobody any of us knew had ever gotten taken in like that. Maybe, if Mrs. Pryor never came back, it would happen. Maybe, if Mrs. Pryor never came back, we wouldn't want to leave the orphanage, even for a farm.

At night, Miss Lillian came around and tucked each of us into bed. She loved us, each and every one of us, just as if we were her own family. We had all been hungry for love for so long. We were starving for it, even more than for good food. When Miss Lillian tucked Nellie in, I heard my friend say "I always wanted my mother to tuck me in."

"She didn't?" Miss Lillian asked.

"No," Nellie replied, "She died when I was little."

Nellie had told me that her mother was beautiful, like a princess, and she used to have a photograph of her in her old house.

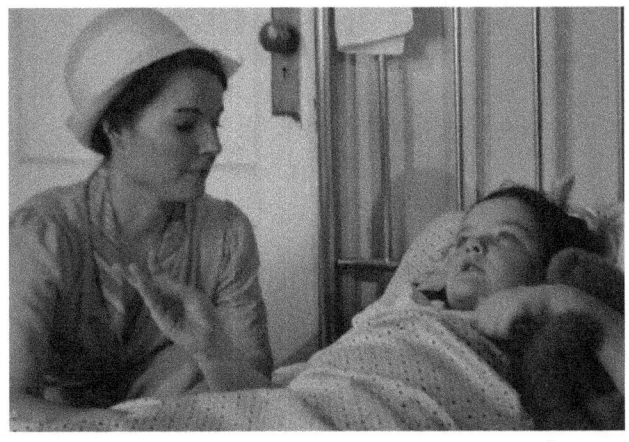

"I'm so sorry," Miss Lillian said. "Did anyone check on you?"

"Daddy did, every night." Nellie said. She sounded upset, but Miss Lillian didn't seem to notice.

"Well, that was nice of him," she said, and I heard Nellie shake her head, her curls rustling against the pillow.

"You needn't worry now," Miss Lillian finally said, and hugged Nellie, then kissed her goodnight. I don't know why Nellie was so upset that her Daddy tucked her in. I love it when Ernie tucks me in.

He came up to check on me later that night. I wasn't asleep. I was afraid that I would have the nightmares again or that someone would get us while we are sleeping.

"I'm scared, Ernie," I told him.

"Be peaceful, little one," he replied, but I didn't feel any better. We weren't safe in our room, not when I could see the bed Anna had died in just on the opposite wall.

"Can't I stay with you tonight?" I asked him. He thought about it for a moment, then shook his head.

"No," he said, "But you and your friend can come down for a cookie, ja?"

I love it when Ernie lets me have a cookie, and Nellie had never been down in his room to get one. They're usually chocolate chip, and he keeps them wrapped up in wax paper tied with string.

"Come on, let's have a cookie," I said, grabbing Nellie's hand, but she looked worried. I finally convinced her, and we both put our shoes on and followed Ernie down to his room in the basement.

"I've never had two princesses visit me at the same time," Ernie said as we went down the last staircase, the one with the green bannister.

It's just a little room, but he keeps all his treasures there. His helmet from the Great War is on the shelf and it has a spike on top of it. The boys don't like Ernie because he was a Kraut. They probably don't know that he has a medal. It is black and silver and shaped like a cross. He polishes his helmet and medal a lot.

On the wall is a half-ripped picture of Mary holding baby Jesus and there is a little framed photo of somebody up on a shelf. He usually has a couple of animal pelts sitting around and there is a big deer's head on the wall. His steamer trunk is on the opposite wall and a scratchy dark blanket is on top of his cot. The curtains on the one little window are half-shredded. Nellie looked suspiciously at the big trap on the floor. Ernie told me once that it is for bears, and then he growled at me and held out his arms like a bear.

I was already sitting on Ernie's cot, swinging my feet, as Nellie walked very slowly into the room and finally sat down beside me. Nellie was hugging her bear tight and playing with her dress.

"Ernie, where's our cookies?" I asked. Sometimes Ernie forgets what he's doing. His face lit up.

"You are right. I promised cookies. I search them," he said, and started to look around the room. Nellie became more and more nervous. I could hear her breathing hard.

"Cookies are here, I know."

Ernie forgets where he puts things, too. He told me once it is because of the gas. He said that he and a bunch of other Kraut soldiers were in a big ditch somewhere when the enemy hit them with gas that made them all sick. Then he had to come to America and live with his uncle because of the gas. America was Ernie's enemy during the war, but not anymore. I wonder what the gas smelled like, and how they hit them with it.

Nellie was rocking back and forth. Ernie noticed she was worried and tried to calm her down, but that only made Nellie more nervous. I don't know why she was being such a baby. Cookies aren't scary. Until Mrs. Pryor went away, they were the only sweets I ever got.

"Once we have cookies," Ernie promised, "we play a little game. Yes... we play a little game." He smiled, but Nellie buried her face in her bear. As soon as he turned to look on the desk, she bolted out the door.

Ernie turned towards her with the cookies that he'd found in his desk, but she was already gone and running up the stairs. He was so disappointed, he almost didn't give me a cookie because he wanted to play with both of us.

Nellie

Ernst is a bad man and Esther doesn't care. He makes the little girls go down to his room with him. I wouldn't stay there, but Esther did, and she plays with him a lot. I know that Anna went down there, too. I saw her sneaking away with him. He's just like my daddy was, but Daddy is dead now and can't hurt anyone anymore.

Esther was outside playing with a great big stick and I went to play with her, but she doesn't like me anymore because I ran away from Ernst. I thought Esther was my friend. I thought she was smarter than Buddy, but she hates me now.

Miss Lillian saw that I was sitting by myself when everyone was playing, so she came over to talk to me. I just had to tell her what had happened. At first, I didn't want to, but she told me I could trust her. We all need somebody to trust. She knows what my Daddy was like. I told her that, I trusted her.

"Esther is mad at me," I said.

"Why?" Miss Lillian knew that Esther and I were always together, and everybody likes Esther.

"Ernst."

"What do you mean, Ernst?" She looked very confused, and glanced at Ernst and the girls playing in the yard. She has to know. How could she not know?

"You have to tell me what you mean. What did Ernst do?" Miss Lillian persisted.

"I don't want to play his cookie game."

She looked worried, but still uncertain.

"What do you mean, cookie game?"

She knew. Everybody knew what Ernst did, and nobody cared.

"You do so! He played it with Anna and he plays it with Esther."

I think she finally understood, and she even looked surprised. She hugged Teddy and me close, but then we heard a car horn honking and the sound of wheels coming up the drive. It was Mrs. Pryor's big black car. Her driver opened the door and we saw her foot, then her leg, then all of her unfold from the back seat. She was wearing a dress so pink it was painful to look at, and a strange hat that made her look like a witch.

"I have returned, children," she proclaimed, and everyone started to gather around her. She wasn't supposed to come back, not ever. Things were better without her, except for Ernst.

Miss Lillian looked down at me.

"I will take care of all of this," she promised, and walked up to Mrs. Pryor, leaving me standing there on the porch, hugging bear. I couldn't hear what they were saying, but Miss Lillian looked worried and Mrs. Pryor looked annoyed. She shook her head "no," and her strange hat bobbed. They called over Esther, who climbed up the porch stairs nervously. Esther's socks have tattered lace on them and her black shoes buckle around her ankles. I watched her feet on each step, saw how her toes pointed just slightly inwards towards each other as Mrs. Pryor and Miss Lillian talked to her. Esther shook her head "no," and Mrs. Pryor asked her another question, but she just kept shaking her head. Miss Lillian looked worried and she and Mrs. Pryor seemed to be arguing. Mrs. Pryor always wins. Just like when my bear got taken away the first time, Miss Lillian couldn't stand up for me. Miss Lillian looked sad and Mrs. Pryor came stomping over towards me, grabbing my arm hard just below my short sleeves. She dragged me into the house.

I thought I knew what she would do to me. When I got in trouble for biting Harmon, she had pulled a wooden spoon out of a drawer in her office.

"Daddy always enjoyed this one," she said, and kissed the spoon. She made me flip my skirt up and pull my panties down and then she smacked me with the spoon, over and over. She was talking to the big picture of the man with the moustache as she hit me.

"Daddy, do you like how your little girl screams? Is she screaming well for you? Scream for Daddy," she told me. I was already crying and yelling. "Scream for Daddy! Scream for Daddy!"

One of the older girls, Betty, said that Mrs. Pryor keeps her daddy's ashes on top of the fireplace in her office, and there was something sitting there that looked like it could be that kind of an urn. When she dragged me in there this time, I stared at the urn. I thought she would get the spoon out of the drawer again, but she didn't.

"I think people should know what you are, don't you? People have a right to know what a little liar you are," Mrs. Pryor said, pushing me down into one of the orange chairs by her desk. Mrs. Baker had sat in one of those chairs when she brought me to the orphanage. She should have kept me at her house. I would have been good, but she hated me. Everybody hates me, even people who pretend to be my friend, like Esther.

I stared at Mrs. Pryor's teeth as she leered at me. I was too scared to talk, but I was afraid of what she would do. She was even angrier this time, and ripped my Teddy from my arms.

"Don't you plead with me," she said, "I know what you are. But others, others might be fooled."

She put her little black purse on the desk, then started to pull off her gloves, a finger at a time, and then with her teeth. Her dress was pink, pink like Esther's dress, but the lipstick she pulled out of her purse was red, like blood.

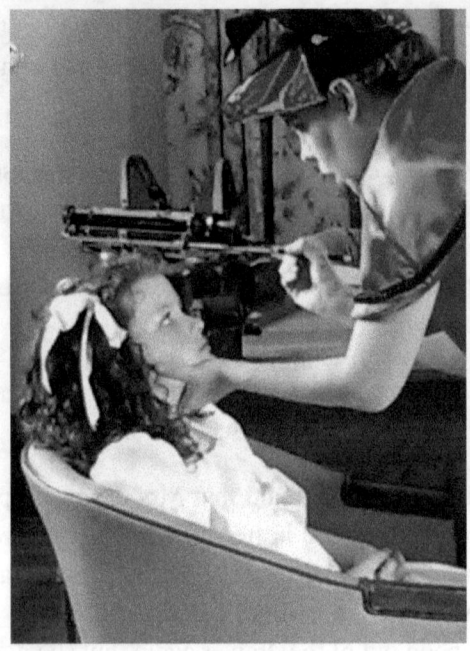

She held me down in the chair and I could feel her covering my mouth with the lipstick, pressing hard against my teeth. I tried to pull away, but she was stronger.

"Hold still while I finish," she said, and slapped me. Then she took something else out of her purse and started to put in on my eyes. It burned and clouded my vision. I was crying now, the hot tears running out of my aching eyes, as Mrs. Pryor's daddy, Mr. Gore, stared from the wall without pity. My bear was watching, too, and he hated Mrs. Pryor, but he couldn't make her stop. Mrs. Pryor opened her compact and showed me my reflection, but I didn't recognize my face. My eyes were rimmed in black, my mouth a red gash. The tears which streamed down my cheeks were black, like soot. I covered my face.

"I think Daddy would have liked you... Yes, daddy would have really liked you. What do you think of your little Jezebel, Daddy?" she asked the picture, then added, "Just the way you like them." In the distance, I heard the footsteps of the other children coming into the house. Mrs. Pryor grabbed my hand.

"Come, we must introduce the children to the real Nellie," she said, as she dragged me away. Everyone was waiting in the work room, and they gathered around as Mrs. Pryor brought me in. She stood in front of the fireplace, holding me against her body, her fingers digging into my shoulders.

"Nellie decided to tell lies," she sneered, "And lies will not be tolerated at Gore Orphanage. Children, what happens to liars?"

"Liar, liar, pants on fire," they all chanted together, their faces distorted and full of rage.

"Yes," Mrs. Pryor said, and I could here joy in her voice, "Liar, liar, pants on fire... that is a very good idea, children. Everyone in a circle!"

She pushed me down onto the floor and the orphans surrounded me, joining hands and spinning around me.

"Liar, liar, pants on fire," they chorused, leaning towards me. I could feel their hot breath. Mrs. Pryor began to laugh.

"Liar, liar, pants on fire," they shouted, and I saw Esther, her face even crueler than the others. Esther wasn't my friend. She hated me. They all hated me.

Mrs. Pryor took the matches down from the mantle and struck one. The flame leapt up between her fingers and she brought it closer and closer to me. She was going to burn me right there, while everyone watched. They all knew what to do. They had done this before, and they were going to burn me, and they would laugh as my skin turned black and fell away from my bones.

"Liar, liar, pants on fire!" they screamed, as I could feel the flame of the match licking at my face.

"Mrs. Pryor!" It was Miss Lillian's voice. The children's cries halted.

"Mrs. Pryor, your brother is on the line."

"Of course. Where are my manners?" Mrs. Pryor asked, shaking out the match, "Off to bed now, children."

They were not children. They were monsters, and they wanted me dead, all of them. They all lined up at the door and only the littlest boy looked back at me, but I could see hate in his eyes, too. Slowly, I got up off the floor and followed them upstairs.

V.

Ernst

Between our trench and the enemy was No-Man's Land. When I close eyes, I see. No-Man's Land, the blasted tree, the arm of the great black gun against the sky. My mind is slow now, and dark, but this I do not forget. I live in No-Man's Land.

I am the Prussian Guard. We are the pride of the people. I am the Prussian Guard because I am tall, and strong. I make my parents proud. I am a good German soldier, and this means I kill many men. I am brave, and they give me a medal. We must be clean and shiny because we are the Prussian Guard and we are brave, so I must polish my Pickelhaube, must make the Wappen, the Eagle, shine. The enemy must see their frightened eyes in the reflection of the Spitze. This is a spike on top of my head. It strikes fear into the enemy.

Before the War, I was a boy. Now I am a man, and I live in No-Man's Land. In the trenches, the rats ate the bodies of the dead. Now, I set my traps for the foxes and bears.

My father was a gamekeeper. His father was a gamekeeper. I was going to be a gamekeeper, but then I became the Prussian Guard and the gas came. My head burst. I heard my mind explode like a bomb, and felt my lungs fill with rot. I could not breathe, and my legs gave way beneath me. They thought I was dead, and I woke up under the bodies of the dead. Their faces were yellow and green. The rats were all around. The bodies of the enemy were hanging in the barbed wire. My mother hangs our clothing like this.

The gas is like fog. It creeps over everything and into everything. It hangs still between my ears, inside the cavern of my mind. The gas slows my thoughts. After the gas, I cannot fight. I am still the Prussian Guard, but I am weak. I am in the hospital.

A little girl brings me flowers and we dance, but I do not know if she is real. I do not know what is real. My hands shake when I shave my face, but I must shave my face because I am the Prussian Guard. I have a medal. I am a great hero, but I am not dead.

They tell me I am not dead. I am glad to know this. They tell me I am Ernst. I remember.

I am a hero, but not here. I am in America now, and they are not the enemy any longer. My uncle is in America, and only he will care for me. I am like a child, they say, but I am large, too large for a child, and I have a medal and a pickelhaube. I know how to trap, and clean pelts, and clean the floor.

They do not like me to speak German here. I learn English. I learn good. My mind is slow, but I can learn. I remember music. When I wake in the morning, I hear it in my head. Marches. Violins. The screams of the shells. All this is music.

He is called Herr Gore. He is good to me. I am an orphan, too, and I am like a child, but large. He gives me Kuchen. Cookies. Cookie time. He tells me I will keep the floor clean and I do. I clean up mess.

The children are sometimes cruel and sometimes kind. They call me cabbage. I do not understand. "Ernst," I tell them. "Kraut, hey Kraut," they say.

I wear my tie. I shave my face. I polish my Pickelhaube and my medal. I give the little girls cookies. They are my friends. They call me Ernie, not cabbage. I show them my medal.

Herr Gore likes to take the little girls into his office. He gives them cookies also. Sometimes they cry. They do not cry when we play a game. I do not want the Kinder to cry.

I keep my knife sharp. Sometimes I find a feather in the woods. Once, it is an eagle feather. We catch fish. I know a song about fish, but I remember only a little. "Die launische Forelle," I sing.

When Herr Gore dies, I am sad. He was my friend. I wear my medal to his funeral because I am a hero, but the people point and me and laugh. Frau Pryor is his daughter and now I work for her. I clean up mess. There is more mess. She does not love Kinder. She does not love Ernst.

Many children come and go. Sometimes they grow up, sometimes they die. I bury the dead ones in the yard and I say a prayer, or as much as I can remember. "Vater unser, unser Vater," I say as the shovel digs. It is like a little trench.

The Polish boy comes to the orphanage. He is skilled with traps. We work together and catch many foxes. I teach him and he does not call me cabbage. He is old, and should go, but he helps me, so he stays. Perhaps he will stay forever and will bury me in the yard when I die.

Anna is a beautiful girl. Her name is a German name, but she is not German. Her hair is very light, like my mother's. She likes to play with me, but then she dies. I clean up mess, but I cry. The children pretend not to see me. My friends do not want to play with me. Frau Pryor thinks I hurt Anna, but I would never hurt her. I promise I will not play with the children any more, but I miss them and they miss me, and then Frau Pryor goes away. Esther screams in the night. In the hospital, after the gas, many men screamed like Esther. She is a little princess, beautiful.

The new girl is beautiful, too, but she hates me. Her hair is black. She does not want to play. Her eyes are like those of a fox, but blue.

I am mopping the stairs. It is hard work and they are never clean because the children go up and down. I sit to wipe my face, and my hand touches something wet. I look at my fingers and they are covered in blood. I stand, and lift the lid of the window seat. There is a dead boy there. His throat is cut. There is a baseball card on his chest.

"Frau Pryor," I say, but she is playing music. I am not allowed to play her piano. She does not have a violin.

I carry the dead boy down the stairs. He weighs very little. His pants are tied with rope instead of a belt because he is very poor. When she sees the dead boy, she is very unhappy.

"No, no, they will shut us down," she says. They cannot shut us down. I think very hard, through the fog in my skull.

"I clean up mess," I tell her.

When I come back, my Polish boy is gone. She says he killed the little ones. I do not believe her. He liked to kill foxes, but not children.

Frau Pryor leaves us with the children and we are kind to them. Lillian says I can buy them a treat, so I buy candy. Children love candy. I buy cookies also. They smile and are happy. We play together, the children, and Lillian, and Ernst. She is very beautiful. She does not call me cabbage. She takes my hand when we are playing and her hand is soft, like the hands of the little girls.

Something changes with Lillian. She becomes afraid of me. I do not understand why. I am a hero, I am the Prussian Guard, but there is a fog of gas in my head.

"Don't you ever touch those girls again!" she hisses between her teeth, but I see her touch them. Why can't I?

Mrs. Pryor talks on the telephone to her brother. He does not come to see us. She tells him she needs more money for an attorney. Then she hangs up the phone and screams loudly, over and over. I cover my ears. When she stops screaming, I look into the office. She is bent over her desk, holding the new girl's toy bear in her arms and crying. I want to touch her, but I am not allowed. I take my bucket to the sink to get more water. I will clean up mess.

I am teaching Ralph to set the traps. We go into the woods together, but he is not as strong as Harmon. He will grow bigger. He is a good boy. I chose him because he wears a tie. His name is very nearly German.

All of the little girls have faces like Maria with the Jesuskind. They love it when I carry them on my back because I am strong and they are small, like birds. Some of them are bigger, but the little ones I like best. They pick flowers and put them on my head. I am large, and I have killed men, but I can be gentle. I want to be gentle, but sometimes I am angry. I am angry that children die and men die and they are my friends. I am angry that I cannot wear my medal because people will laugh at me. I am angry that I cannot play with the Kinder any more.

Cienna Cetera as an orphan girl and Samantha Ziglear as Irene

There was a girl I liked many years ago, but she would not marry me because my head was full of gas. I did not ask her. Her name was Sibylla and she was a princess. I am a hero and have a medal, but I am not well.

There are many things I cannot remember, but this I do remember. Lillian screamed and screamed in the morning. Her scream is lower than Esther's. She was calling for Mrs. Pryor, but I was nearby, so I went up the stairs and there she was, crouching on the landing beside something small and bloody.

"Go away," she hissed when she saw me, but I know who is dead now. It is my Esther, my little princess Esther. I see her tiny arm, her beautiful hair. I go away, but I come back again after Miss Lillian and Mrs. Pryor go away.

I take little Esther into my arms and her head falls from side to side. One side is purple and red, like a man choking on the gas. She is so very small. The tears fall down my cheeks. The Polish boy is gone, so I bury her alone, beneath a large tree where the wind will sing to her. "Schlaf, Kindlein, schlaf," the tree will sing, and I remember another song, "Schlaf in himmlischer Ruh."

"Vater unser, unser Vater," I pray. In my pocket, I have some candy. I put it in the little trench with my Esther. I kiss her goodnight.

I clean up mess.

Lillian

Something is terribly wrong in this place. Three children are dead, and no one knows why. Ernst has apparently been molesting children, and possibly even killing them. When Anna died, I thought she had simply slipped away in her sleep, but Buddy's death could have been nothing but murder. I loved that little boy, loved his innocence and goodness, and someone slit his throat and hid his body. Mrs. Pryor believed it was Harmon, and she took him away somewhere. It is not my place to ask where.

He was a cruel child, fond of trapping animals and giving the other boys black eyes, but I had thought him a bully and nothing more. We tried to make the children forget, Ernst and I, while Mrs. Pryor was away. We treated them with love and kindness and I watched them blossom. Even Nellie, who was always so reserved and cautious, began to open up.

That little girl has been horribly abused, first by her father and now, apparently, by Ernst. Esther denied everything Nellie told me, but it all makes sense. She said he had been abusing Anna, too. I am disgusted. He is a simpleton, but he does know right from wrong. I thought he loved the children, but he has been hurting them. It is vile and disgusting.

The worst of it, though, is little Esther. Her tiny body was crumpled on the back steps, her head oozing blood. It looked as if she had fallen down the stairs, but how? She should have been safely locked in her room, not wandering the halls in the early hours of the morning.

I love these children fiercely. They are they only children I will ever have. They have lost their parents, and no one shows them love but me. But someone is killing them, and I am deathly afraid, especially for Nellie.

Buddy and Esther were her best friends, and now both of them are dead. I may lose my job in the process, but I intend to save her. Mrs. Pryor doesn't care for the children at all. She never wanted to run the orphanage, but it was what her wealthy father left her as an inheritance. Mrs. Pryor is blighted inside. I know she steals their money and spends it on herself. She hardly pays me anything, but I stay for the sake of the children.

I was so thankful that Schoolboy Rowe could come here, but she made a debacle of that. I could tell that she was enamored of him and it was disgusting. She must be nearly twice his age. When she was screaming at Harmon to hit Buddy, I could feel Mr. Rowe's embarrassment. Mrs. Pryor humiliated me, but I should not have been surprised. When Harmon was younger, she used to hang him and Mikey from coat hooks and make them swing at each other. If he grew up to be a monster, it's no wonder.

That morning, after I found Esther's pitiful little body, I went up to the children's room and, waking Nellie, drew her into the bathroom.

"I've got to get you out of here," I told her, and she looked up at me eagerly, innocently, with those beautiful pale blue eyes which are always so striking with her dark hair. I didn't want to tell her, but I had to. She needed to understand why we had to escape, but why we had to be careful, too. "I've got bad news," I said, as gently as I could, "Esther is dead."

How do you tell a little girl whose whole family has died of food poisoning, who has been sexually abused by two men, that her best friend has died? Simply, clearly.

"How?" she asked. She has been so quiet and withdrawn, especially since Buddy died, and Mrs. Pryor has been very hard on her. She's been holding it all inside. She didn't cry, but I didn't expect her to. I could never have anticipated what she did, though. She took her teddy bear in both hands and started moving it from side to side, making strange sounds with her mouth.

"Boom, boom, boom, crash," she said, and hit the bear's head against the sink. She did it again and again. Horrified, I reached out to her.

"You must be in shock, dear," I said, but she wouldn't stop. The bear was taken through its terrible paces again.

"Was it like this?" Boom, boom, boom, crash, "Or like this?"

"What?" was all I could manage to say.

"How Esther died. Did she fall to the right or to the left?"

The poor child was falling apart before my eyes, yet she seemed so terribly calm.

"Does it matter?" I said, a trifle too harshly, perhaps. "She's dead and I've got to get you to safety."

Nellie looked up at me again and my heart broke for her.

"Nowhere is safe," she said simply, and I could see that, for this little girl, no place had ever been. I would take her to my parents and we would raise her in peace and safety. Nothing would ever harm her again. She would be my little girl, and their granddaughter, and we would put all of this behind us. We would be protected, because I had done what Mrs. Pryor had refused to do. When she left the office, I took up the telephone and called the police. I reported the suspicious deaths, all of them. The children had to be protected.

"I called the police. They will figure out who is killing all of the children," I told Nellie, and her eyes grew even wider.

"How?" she asked.

"Science," I said. "They can check for fingerprints. It's going to be all right." I held her close, and felt her trembling. "Listen to me," I said, looking into her eyes, "We have to act like everything is normal until they arrive tomorrow."

"Yes, Miss Lillian," she said, as if I had asked her to fetch my coffee, then walked out of the bathroom, holding her bear under her arm.

I looked at myself in the mirror, searching my own face for signs of weakness.

"You can do this, Lillian," I told my frightened reflection, "You can do this. You are a strong, modern woman."

Nellie kept looking at me all day, as we worked on an order of moss roses. I kept her behind as the other children went up for supper,

82

ostensibly to clean the room, but really to talk with her. Mrs. Pryor came in just as the girls were leaving, though, so I set Nellie to dusting with a rag. I was able to whisper to her, though.

"The police will be here first thing in the morning." She nodded, and I went back to where Mrs. Pryor sat at the work table. She would be in a chatty mood today, the one day when I least wanted to speak with her. She was going out that night, and was already dressed in a seafoam green silk gown which the girls had made for her.

"I can't believe that Esther was so careless," she said, her face careworn. "She was such a good child."

Perhaps somewhere, deep in her cold heart, she had cared a little. I don't believe it was an accident, but I couldn't tell her that. For all I know, perhaps Mrs. Pryor is the one responsible.

"We need to take precautions to keep the children safe," I said. It was all I could do for them now, until the police came.

"Just as long as they are inexpensive," she replied, callously, "I can't afford more unforeseen expenditures."

Her mind is always on money, and never on their welfare.

"I will try to find a way to keep them safe, without any additional cost." I had already done so, but she didn't know it. Perhaps they would be sent to a county home, or maybe they would be given families. I would do whatever necessary to keep Nellie myself, and perhaps one or two of the others, also. They were all such lovely children, but so neglected, clinging to life like little seedlings sprouting among rocks.

"Good," said Mrs. Pryor, "there might even be a bonus in it for you."

I smiled, astonished yet again at the workings of her mind. Nellie came up to the table, shifting from foot to foot as she stood awkwardly waiting for acknowledgement.

"What is it, Nellie?" Mrs. Pryor asked.

"I just wanted to know if Miss Lillian would like some coffee," she said, but her inflections were strange and stilted. The poor child was trying to act normal, but I could only imagine how frightened she must be.

"Of course, Nellie," I said, smiling at her.

"Can I get you some coffee also, Mrs. Pryor?" she asked in that odd, pinched voice.

Mrs. Pryor and I gave her our cups and she walked, slowly and carefully, across the room to the percolator.

"She seems to have finally learned some manners," Mrs. Pryor noted, watching her pour the coffee.

"She is a good girl," I responded. "She just needs time to adjust."

"I think you may be right," Mrs. Pryor said, then sighed. "I will be so happy when things return to normal here."

There can never be a normal here again, I thought, not after all that has happened.

"This orphanage could be such a godsend for the children," I said, and imagined a place where the orphans could be loved and nourished.

"Only if it turned a profit," Mrs. Pryor countered. Nothing could be better for them than to take them away from her.

Nellie had returned with two steaming cups of coffee, and place them gently on the table.

"There you go," she said, just as stiffly as before.

"Thank you," I told her with a special smile, and took a sip of the coffee.

"Mrs. Pryor, can I go to my room now? I'm very tired," she said suddenly, and I was relieved. She would go to sleep, Mrs. Pryor would suspect nothing, and in the morning, the police would come.

"What a wonderful idea," Mrs. Pryor replied.

Nellie dropped a little curtsey, thanked Mrs. Pryor, and trotted out of the room. I remembered that her family had been European, and cultured, despite the abuse she had endured. Somewhere underneath, she was a charming little girl. My parents would love her.

"I believe discipline is finally changing her for the better," Mrs. Pryor said, and I nodded, but I had started feeling odd. All the pressure of the situation was finally taking its toll on me.

"Have you ever considered that love might be more effective?" I countered. I was being awfully bold, but who could know what the police might do. Perhaps Mrs. Pryor would be left in charge of the children.

"Children are like animals," she responded cynically. "They will rebel the moment they sense weakness."

I felt a terrible pain in my stomach and the room was spinning.

"I don't feel well," I muttered, placing the cup back on the table.

"It's probably all the excitement," Mrs. Pryor said. "Relax. My attorney has assured me that everything will be fine."

Of course she had an attorney. I hadn't thought of that, but I felt so ill that I could barely register her words.

"My stomach is hurting," I told her. Perhaps I had appendicitis. Once of the children had died of that, once.

"Drink some more," Mrs. Pryor said, lifting up the coffee cup. I took another sip.

"Better?"

I nodded. "I think so. This coffee has a nice zing to it."

"Really? Let me try it."

Mrs. Pryor took a sip.

"You are quite correct. Very tasty."

The room was spinning again, even more violently. I put my hand to my head.

"I feel dizzy," I said, and my voice sounded far away.

"Are you angling for another day off?"

"No… I think it's…"

Everything had suddenly become clear. I was such a fool. The answer had been before my eyes all along, but I had refused it see it. I tried to stand, but my legs were gone and I fell to the floor.

"It was she," I said to Mrs. Pryor, though I could barely form the words. She had to know. She had to save the children.

"Who?"

"Nellie. But why…"

I was seized with sudden, unbearable pain. I felt my body tremble, convulse, and then nothing. I was a light on the ceiling, looking down at myself and Mrs. Pryor. I saw that my hat had fallen from my head.

Mrs. Pryor

Where had she gone? The little beast had poisoned Lillian, who was lying dead on the floor, and I had taken several sips, as well. How much would it take? My vision was already becoming blurred, but I pulled myself up and stumbled into the hall. I could hear movement somewhere.

I should have known from the moment I saw her devil eyes that she was worse than all of Daddy's little trollops. They had regarded me with saucy insolence, secure in their knowledge that he loved them better than me, but Nellie... the dainty white dress and blue ribbons had never been quite enough to disguise her inhumanity. Her eyes were always those of a cornered predator. I was right to punish her. I should have had Ernst drown her in a sack of rocks, like an unwanted kitten.

How many had she killed? Buddy, surely. Esther? Anna? Her parents? I had blamed that boy, that strong and handsome boy, and would not listen to a word of his defense. I should have known better. I would not let her kill me, not until I had taken my revenge. Lillian had always been fragile in both mind and body, but I am strong. I will close my hands around Nellie's throat.

"Whore... whore... Victoria Gore Pryor does not die to a little whore!" I screamed. I felt the woodwork of the doorframe and made my way into the hall. I heard a metallic jangling and a flash of white raced past me, slipping through my grasp as I fell headlong towards the stairs. She had the keys and she was laughing.

I started to crawl up the stairs, but my feet were tangled in my gown and I could hear the silk tearing. The stairs were vibrating—heavy footsteps—and then Ernst was by my side. He is all I have left, and he is strong, but feeble-minded.

"She's trying to kill me," I told him. I could no longer see his face clearly, my eyes were dimming more and more, but I expect he wore his typical expression of dull confusion.

"Be peaceful," the great lout said, and I wanted to claw at him until my words would penetrate his thick skull.

"Miss Lillian is already dead," I said, pointing into the room where her body lay sprawled across the floorboards. I heard him gasp. Good. I was getting somewhere with him at last, and there was so little time. He had seen Nellie at the top of the stairs, and the wheels were ever so slowly turning in his mind. Like the gears of a great tower clock, then began to groan into motion.

"It can't be the little girl. Little girls don't kill."

"She killed them all," I began, but was overcome by a wave of the most intense stomach pain and nausea imaginable and retched over the bannister. Ernst caught me as I fell and he lifted me as easily as he would lift a child. My body was failing me, but Ernst had enough power in his limbs for us both. I rested my face against the coarse cloth of his overalls. He smelled of aftershave and wood smoke. I could no longer tell for certain if my eyes were open or closed; I lifted my recalcitrant fingers to my face and felt the encircling rim of my eyelashes. Open. I was blind.

I felt us descend, heard the creaking of the stairs, and then Ernst lay me tenderly on his cot.

"It never was you, was it?" I asked him, feeling for his cheek.

"I never hurt the Kinder," he said solemnly. He was no more than a great child himself, and I had believed the worst of him.

"How could I have been so blind?"

"I go clean up mess," I heard him say in that slow, halting voice. It is what he has always done, clean up the messes. I realize he has always guarded me fiercely, and for this I love him.

"Here," he said, placing something in my outstretched hand, "Cookie."

I reached for him, caressed him.

"You're a good boy, Ernst."

"Save the Kinder," he said suddenly. He had understood at last. "Save the Kinder..." I heard his heavy footfalls as he left the room. I could rest now. Ernst would be our savior, would clean up the mess. The cookie slipped from my fingers as I lay back on his narrow bed.

I heard footsteps above me, the little ones of the monster child and the heavy ones of Ernst. He was pursuing her, he would catch her in his snares like he did the animals of the forest. Perhaps he would skin her and boil her bones.

I sensed him entering the room again, coming close, bending over me.

"Is that you, Ernst?"

He said nothing. I took his hand.

"Good boy. I was wrong about you. I should never have taken that little tramp in."

His hand pulled away. He loved all little girls, and did not understand. He must be made to understand.

"Just catch that little whore for me... I will give you extra cookies."

He was gone from my side, and I heard movement. Papers were rustling, flying about the room.

"What is all that racket?"

Something was very wrong. I tried to lift myself up, stretched out my arms. My nostrils began to prickle.

"What's that smell?" I felt the arm of Ernst's chair then, as I moved to the left, a sudden warmth.

"That's fire... oh no..." I lunged toward the rustling and my fingers brushed something small and soft. I heard her laughing at me. Over and over, the demented giggling of the murderous child.

"Little Jezebel!" I was crawling along, using Ernst's desk for support, when suddenly something gave way beneath my fingers and I fell hard onto the floor, screaming. I could not rise again, even as the flames licked at the hem of my silk gown.

Nellie

They all deserved to die. I had my doubts about Miss Lillian, thought about escaping with her, but she called the police. Teddy said I couldn't trust her. I couldn't trust anyone but him. Esther and Buddy pretended to be my friends, but my bear is my only real friend. I saw Miss Lillian talking to Mrs. Pryor and smiling. She knew what I had done, so I dumped the rat poison in her coffee, too. No one really likes me, no one except Teddy.

Poison is so much easier that other ways. It is good for a little girl like me. My daddy hurt me and my stepmother hated me, so I poisoned them both. My brother had to die, too, because they all ate together. I was sent to my room without supper. That's why I survived and they are dead.

As soon as I left the work room, I skipped a little down the hall out of sheer joy. It had all gone perfectly. I watched from behind the columns in the foyer. As soon as Miss Lillian was down on the floor, I skipped into Mrs. Pryor's office. It took a little while to find her big ring of keys in the last desk drawer and she was staggering out into the hallway when I passed her, but I could see that she would die soon, too, and couldn't catch me, so I skipped right past her as she called me all those dirty names.

I needed the keys to lock the orphans in the bedroom. It was easy. They didn't even notice. I went down the back stairs to find Ernst, but he wasn't in his room. Mrs. Pryor was there instead, and she was still alive. I went right up to her and she couldn't see me. She thought I was Ernst, but she had sent him to get me and she just wouldn't die. She called me a little Jezebel again, and I know what that means. My brows knitted together. When I am angry, people die.

I threw all the papers together in a corner, then lit one of the matches I have been carrying. I stole them a while ago and always use them to light my lantern. It was funny to see her blind and helpless, stretching out her bare arms in that awful green dress that was so hard to make. Teddy and I laughed and laughed, and laughed even more when she grabbed the fox pelt instead of the desk and fell over. I wanted to see her die, but the smoke was choking me and I had to run away.

We had planned it for a long time. "Burn the house down," Teddy had told me. I wanted to know what burning flesh smells like. Is it like bacon?

Ernst was the only problem left, but he would be difficult because of his size. I had hoped to sneak up on him asleep and let Teddy sit on his face, like I did with Anna, but he was awake and looking for me instead. Anna had kicked a little bit, but Teddy smiled at me when it was over. I knew they would blame either Harmon or Ernst. I had seen them both looking at her.

Buddy had to die because he had squealed on me. I woke him up in the night, telling him that I'd found his baseball card and asking him to come with me to get them. "It's an adventure," he said with a big smile. "Yes Buddy, an adventure," I told him, and we crawled out through the bathroom closet and sneaked down the back stairs to the kitchen. I showed him the card and slit his throat with Mrs. Pryor's letter opener. His last words were, "That's not very nice." I liked Buddy, but he shouldn't have squealed on us.

"Look what he did to your dress," Teddy told me, and I realized there was blood on my skirt. Buddy had always been messy. We dragged his body down the stairs, his feet in their square-toed black shoes bouncing off each step, and I stuffed him in the window seat where he'd hidden his treasures. I gave him back his Schoolboy Rowe baseball card, laying it on his chest. Having to kill Buddy made me a little sad, but Teddy reminded me that he hadn't really been my friend. "Never trust, never care" was our motto. We washed out my dress in the bathtub and scrubbed it with soap, but a little stain remained. Nobody noticed.

Esther had betrayed me, too, just like Buddy, so I told her that I'd talked to Ernst and we were all going to play together. Then I gave her a shove on the back stairs. Her head bounced off the door jamb and she looked back at me for a moment, confused, blood trickling into her hair. I gave her another push, harder this time, and she sailed down the stairs. She was a scrawny little girl and it hardly took any strength at all to shove her.

Smoke was beginning to rise up from the basement, filling the second floor of the orphanage. I could hear Ernst's heavy footfalls before I could see him, and he was calling my name. It was easy to dance through the haze-filled halls, skip up the steps, and elude him at every turn. As the smoke continued to rise, it seeped under the door of the orphans' bedroom.

"It's smoke!" I heard someone say, and they began pounding on the door and screaming for Miss Lillian, Mrs. Pryor, and Ernst. I smiled. The dormitory room is in the attic. There is no other way out.

I heard Ernst come crashing up the front stairs, so I hid on the first landing of the back staircase. He stopped at the bedroom door.

"I get you out!" Ernst shouted, tugging on the door.

"It's locked!" the children yelled back, panicked. It sounded as if they were all at the door, pounding from the inside. I imagined them, trampling each other in futile panic, and held my bear up to my face to stifle my giggles.

"The keys!" Ernst had a sudden thought, and I realized for certain how stupid he is. Outwitting him would not be a challenge, but it would be a very enjoyable game for a little while. We would play together, and then he would die. He raced back down the front stairs, all the way down to Mrs. Pryor's office, and I skipped down the back stairs. The smoke there was becoming thicker, and I began to cough, then held Teddy up to my face to help shield mouth and nose. I could hear Ernst emptying the drawers in the desk, throwing things all over the office. I giggled, then shook the keys. He didn't hear, so I crept closer and shook them again.

"Nellie!" he said, and I took off running, jingling the keys. Once on the stairs, he lunged for them and I felt his fingers brush the key ring, but I skipped away as he tripped. Murder is fun, Teddy told me, and he was right.

Inferno

Irene and Ralph were the first children to notice something was wrong. They had heard piercing screams from somewhere below, and moments later, the sound of the key in the lock. They had wanted to believe that Mrs. Pryor was keeping them safe in their room, but them the smoke started to creep under the door, billowing silently across the warped floor of the dormitory.

They began to pound on the door and their panic attracted the other children, who began to cluster around the door, pressing their bodies against the heavy oaken panel. One little boy was pounding on the wall beside the door, screaming "Help us!" again and again.

They heard Ernst outside the door, but he was only there for a moment before racing off again in search of the keys. They did not know that Miss Lillian lay dead of poison in the workroom below or that Mrs. Pryor's body had helped to feed the flames at their source. Below them, it spread along the wooden joists of the house, creeping ever closer.

Panic spreads as quickly as fire, and soon children were rushing madly around the room, seeking desperately for any possible egress. Two of the older boys yanked on the large window above the portico roof until they finally forced it open. An acrid plume of smoke flooded through the open window, full into their faces, and they fell to the floor, choking. Mae bent over the boys, calling their names, shaking their shoulders, and weeping hysterically. They were the first to fall.

Three of the older girls stood on the window seat in one of the dormers, pounding their fists against the glass and screaming in wordless hysteria. As the smoke poured in from the portico window, they began to cough and choke. One of them, overcome by a fit of coughing, knelt for a moment. When she lifted her head again, both of her friends lay motionless on the floor. She screamed for a few moments and then she, too, was silent.

Near the door, the remaining children piled on top of each other, clawing at the wood. One boy in a blue plaid shirt already lay immobile on the floor—whether he had been suffocated in the crush of bodies or by the smoke was impossible to tell. Some of the smaller children had been trampled in the panic and, pressed to the floor, had lost consciousness as they were submerged in the thick carpet of smoke.

They heard Ernst's footsteps descending the stairs.

"Don't leave us!" the orphans screamed. The little blond boy's fists were growing bloody, but still he pounded on the wall.

"Don't let us die!" cried those who could still find words. Others merely shrieked, over and over.

When Ernst came again, he carried a fire extinguisher, but the danger to the children in the dormitory room was not yet flame—this had not spread to the top floor of the orphanage. Rather, it was the creeping smoke which had already claimed several of the children. Just a few inches of wood separated the huddled mass of children from Ernst, who was attempting to use the copper fire extinguisher as a battering ram. Once, twice, three times he threw the whole force of his powerful body at the door, but it did not budge.

The door was set on its hinges to open into the dormitory room. In their fear and panic, the children had barricaded the door from the inside with their own bodies.

Nellie danced through the house, shaking the keys like a tambourine. Her pale blue eyes were bright above the bear she held over her mouth and nose. She skipped through the halls in celebration. They had hurt her, all of them, and now they would suffer. "Liar, liar, pants on fire," they had screamed at her. It was in that moment that she had planned her revenge.

Ernst was in hot pursuit of Nellie, but he could no longer see her in the thickening smoke. Her demonic laughter rang through the halls, and she seemed to be everywhere and nowhere. He threw open the door of the dining room. It was filled with crackling and dancing flames and the heat singed his eyebrows. He threw the door closed again and leaned, gasping, over the railing. Below him, he heard the jingle of the keys. The lights below had been masked by the black, smothering billows of smoke. He could see nothing, but pursued the sound. She was there, and she had the keys. He had only to find one small girl to rescue all of the Kinder, but the smoke seared his lungs like the gas he had once breathed in the trenches of the Great War. The screams of the children above echoed throughout the house— inhuman shrieks of despair.

Willow Conley as an orphan girl

Ernst ran again up the stairs to the door of the dormitory, throwing himself again and again at the door. He knew time was running out. Already, their cries were growing fainter, the voices fewer. He was the Prussian guard, he was a hero with a medal, but he could not save them.

One of the twins was already silent. Her sister, who had never been alone for a moment in her life, regarded her in mute horror for a moment, then redoubled her screaming. She had seen her own fate, beheld her own body lying there. They were so alike that most of the children could not tell one from the other. They had slept in the same bed, fingers entwined, every night of their ten years. Soon, they would lie together in death, but in this searing moment, each was alone.

They were falling rapidly now inside the dormitory, and only a few children remained conscious. The little bodies were strewn on the floor, heaped beside the door.

In the hallway, Ernst thought of the children, one by one. First the boys, big and small, who had set traps with him in the woods and caught fish among the rocks, then the beautiful princesses, fair and dark, tall and short. He remembered his Anna and Esther, such precious girls, gone already. "Schlaf, Kindlein, schlaf," he thought, "May they all sleep peaceful." Ernst slid down the door, then pressed his hand against it. They were there, so very near, yet beyond his grasp.

"Listen to me, Kinder," he said, gasping for air as the dense smoke permeated his lungs, "I am here. I will not leave you. I will never leave you. Never..."

Ralph and Irene heard Ernst's soothing voice, and then silence from beyond the door. He had been their comforter, their lifeline, and now he was gone. Irene looked around at the shadowy forms of her friends lying still under the rolling blanket of smoke. Slowly, her body went limp.

Ralph was still pounding on the door, screaming, when he suddenly realized that his was the only human voice amid the groaning of the timbers and the cracking of the flames. He coughed for a moment, and then all was silent within Gore Orphanage.

The night sky glowed above the trees surrounding the orphanage, and the windows of the building were already filled with dancing red and orange tongues of flame when the front door opened and Nellie, clutching her bear, walked out into the night. She paused for a moment, smiled, then skipped away. Moments later, the roof of the orphanage collapsed and the whole structure was consumed in purging flames.

Aftermath: Epilogue

Grandma Nellie and Amber were securely fastened in the back of the family sedan as Ted drove them towards his mother's house. He looked up for a moment as the car passed under the overpass reading "Gore Orphanage Road," then glanced in the rearview mirror.

Grandma Nellie's pale blue eyes were unnaturally bright in her wrinkled face. She had seen the sign, too, and heaven only knew what dark memories it had stirred in her.

Amber was all dressed up for the occasion, her beautiful blonde hair pulled back with white barrettes trimmed with net and rhinestones. They matched her shoes, which were white with sparkly bows. Her dress was blue with a white daisy print. Grandma Nellie's shirt was blue and white, too. They'd planned their outfits together.

Amber had been whispering in her teddy bear's ear and giggling as Grandma Nellie looked on with a wistful smile. Sarah sat morosely in the front seat. She'd begged her daughter to leave the smelly old bear at home, but Amber had insisted that Bear was a part of the family, too, and had to come along.

"He'll be very angry if we leave him at home," she had warned.

Ted wondered if Amber's obsession with the bear was fueled, in part, by the relative paucity of men in their family. His own father was long dead, and his grandfather had never been a part of his life, or his mother's. All he knew was that his name had been Harmon and he'd been in trouble with the law. Grandma Nellie had known him as a girl, and then they met again when she was a teenager and living with a foster family after the orphanage burned down, but he was a feckless character who hadn't stayed around to raise his daughter.

"I love Bear," Amber said, kissing the matted fur of her toy's forehead.

"And I love you, Amber dearie," Grandma Nellie said, stroking Amber's hair.

Ted smiled hopefully.

"You know, Grandma, you can be a real sweetie at times," he said.

Grandma Nellie's blue eyes sparkled.

"I am whatever I need to be," she replied.

Author's Postscript

Some stories haunt the imagination. The tale of the children who perished in the Gore Orphanage fire, and whose spirits still haunt the woods of Vermilion, Ohio, has been a favorite scary story of generations of northern Ohioans. Like many such tales, its origins have been obscured in years of retelling and the various versions do not always accord with each other.

In telling our version of the Gore Orphanage story, first in film and now in this novel, Cody Knotts and I chose to add a number of details and alter others. It was never our intent to present either a scholarly study of folkloric traditions or an historical account of Rev. Sprunger and the Light of Hope Orphanage, or the Swift Mansion/Rosedale, or the Collinwood School Fire, all of which contributed to the legend. Rather, we chose to create a work of historical fiction set in the Great Depression which explores issues of child abuse, mistaken perceptions, the delicate business of raising children well, and the destructive power of fire.

My husband, filmmaker Cody Knotts, and I first encountered Gore Orphanage through a serendipitous—one might even say fateful—encounter with a Gore Orphanage Road sign on an overpass. We were returning from signing a contract with a band in Detroit, *Dead in 5,* for Cody's film *Pro Wrestlers vs. Zombies* and somehow found ourselves on a route which passed under this sign. Why and how we were there we could never later determine, as it should not have been part of our route. I was ill with an untreated and very powerful sinus infection, and through the haze of congestion and fever, I thought "That would be an incredible title for a film." Whipping out my phone to determine how such a name would arise, I found both accounts of the legend and its debunking. Cody and I began to discuss the story in the car, and the plot of the film started to form in my mind. We knew from the start that we did not want to create a "found footage, teens in the woods" feature, but rather an origin story about how the fire had been set and why the ghosts of the children remained, endlessly screaming in the woods.

At the film's center, I decided, would be two women, or rather a woman and a girl—the director of the orphanage and an orphan named Nellie. While we maintained the "Old Man Gore" character which had appeared in some tellings of the legend as the orphanage director, we made him a wealthy turn-of-the-century industrialist who, like Andrew Carnegie, had risen from obscure beginnings and later given back to those less fortunate than himself. Victoria Gore Pryor, his daughter, was the unwilling inheritor of her father's legacy who took out her frustrated ambitions and blighted dreams on the children.

Nellie, in her hair ribbons and white dress, was part of my vision from the start. I knew that, despite her perceived innocence, she would be the party responsible for the conflagration, and that those children would not be her first victims. Still in the car on the way back from Detroit, I began to research little girls who kill and found the case of Mary Bell, a young British girl who had murdered other children. Mary's dark hair and blue eyes were very reminiscent of a young actress whom Cody had worked with previously, Emma Leigh Smith. We had found our Nellie, and Cody's prior study of criminal psychology and the traits of sociopaths helped to flesh out the character.

Ernst, the German janitor, was inspired by a figure in the Collinwood School Fire accounts. Fritz Hirter, the Swiss-German custodian of the school, was first blamed for the tragic fire, and then later revealed to be a hero who had tried to rescue the children. While we considered a whole host of actors for this pivotal role, a figure from Cody's past—entrepreneur Bill Townsend—expressed interest and gave an excellent audition by Skype. Only after shooting the film did we realize that Bill's mother, Jackie Mayer, was an icon in the Gore Orphanage area as a Miss America from nearby Sandusky.

Mrs. Pryor was, by far, the hardest role to fill. Several well-known actresses expressed interest after reading the script and at one point, we even thought we had filled the role with someone whom I thought was perfect—she looked as I had envisioned and, when we spoke on the phone, understood the complex motivations of the character and how she needed to come across to the audience. However, a change in her shooting schedule for a TV series left us scrambling to find a Mrs. Pryor with only weeks before principal photography was to begin. We posted an audition notice on an online casting service, but also began pursuing actresses across the globe who had portrayed Lady Macbeth. While we received several strong auditions, our Mrs. Pryor was finally found through the online casting site when we received Maria Olsen's submission. Maria brought everything we had imagined—and more—to the role, especially in her interpretation of Mrs. Pryor's relationship with her father.

Miss Lillian was created to present a more sympathetic adult who cares about the children and tries to protect them in the face of evil. Cody had long wanted to work with actress and TV personality Keri Maletto, and we were thrilled when she agreed to play Miss Lillian.

We found "Gore Bear," as we referred to the teddy, at an antique shop in Whitby, England, while there for the first screening of *Pro Wrestlers vs. Zombies* at the Bram Stoker International Film Festival. Bit by bit, we began to piece together the script and the cast.

Shooting in Scottdale, Pennsylvania, and on location in Northern Ohio during the summer of 2014, we did what independent filmmakers are always advised against undertaking; we made a period piece starring children. The young actors and their families were outstandingly dedicated to the project, despite stifling heat and the lack of working bathrooms in the primary location and swarms of mosquitos in the Ohio locations. During a break in filming, Maria,

Cody, several carloads of young actors (or "Gorphans," as they had become known on set), and I returned to Vermilion to visit the supposed site of the orphanage, as had many legend trippers before us. I was struck by its isolation, even today, and the sharp rocky cliff faces and rushing water which surrounded it.

The characters we had created had become so real in my mind by the end of filming that each had developed an extensive backstory, shaped both by my own imagination and discussions with the actors. To tell these stories, I felt the novel had to be written. The original screen treatment had been my work. Cody had fleshed it out into a script which had impressed and attracted nearly everyone who read it, and now the story was passed to me again to transform into a book. Like an urban legend, details metamorphosed with each retelling.

The people of northern Ohio, for whom the tale of Gore Orphanage, in all its varied forms, has been a part of life, will recognize certain key aspects—the fire, the screaming children, the abusive orphanage director, the bully, and even the laundry in the cooking pot—but others were cut from the whole cloth of my imagination. Like all truly powerful myths, it explores primal urges and fears which rest somewhere deep within each of us.

Emily Lapisardi

May 2015

About the Author

Emily Lapisardi is also the director of *Gore Orphanage*, a feature film which premiered in the summer of 2015. She is currently pursuing a master's degree in sacred music at Duquesne University and holds a bachelor's of music in vocal performance from West Virginia University, where she was named both Honors College J. and C. Nath Outstanding Senior and WVU Foundation Outstanding Senior, and received the university's nomination for both the Rhodes and Marshall Scholarships. She has performed as a singer, pianist, and organist in both the United States and Europe, having been selected by audition to attend prestigious training programs including the Ezio Pinza Council for American Singers of Opera in Italy, the American Institute of Musical Studies in Austria, and the American Singers' Opera Project in North Carolina. As a musicologist, she has studied the music of the Harmony Society, a German communal religious group residing in Pennsylvania and Indiana in the nineteenth century, received a research fellowship for her work on Harmonist hymnody from the Communal Studies Association, and published articles on the Harmonists in several journals. She also presents first-person portrayals of historical figures for museums, historical societies, and educational institutions throughout the United States; past venues have included the International Spy Museum, Heinz History Center, and several National Park Service sites. She resides in southwestern Pennsylvania with her husband, filmmaker Cody Knotts, and cats Claudius and Calpurnia.

Gore Orphanage